Whole Cloth

Whole Cloth

12 Short Stories

Charles Ohrenschall

Celestial Fire
an imprint of Teleios Counseling Ministries

This is a work of fiction. Names, characters, places, and incidents are the product of the author's imagination or are used fictitiously, and any resemblance to actual persons, living or dead, is entirely coincidental.

ISBN-10: 0615936792
ISBN-13: 978-0615936796

For:

PNO
EMO
CRO

and of course

EWO

Contents

Acknowledgements / ix

Introduction / xi

A Worthy Son / 1

The Abba of Sawtooth Mountains / 19

My Grandpaw Kearns / 33

Fighting Dragons / 39

The Boy Who Flew Too Close to the Sun / 55

The Sacrifice / 65

Mattie / 79

Christmas Story / 95

The Lion and the Hyena / 113

Pastorale / 127

The Wound Licker / 133

Journal of the Plague Year / 165

About the Author / 201

Acknowledgements

My grateful thanks to the lovely and talented Joline Falco, who listened to my vision of what this book's cover should look like, and then did her computer magic so that it did.

Many thanks to Chris Tiegreen and Len Sykes, who read several of these stories and gave me valuable, and encouraging, feedback.

Thanks to the gracious lady from Rome (Georgia) whom I met several years ago at a square dance. She gave me permission to use her somewhat unusual name in my stories. So I'm thinking, Margene, that you may also appear in some of my future stories.

Finally, my heartfelt thanks and love to Patsy: I couldn't have done this without you. You have had such a large part in helping me become who I am today.

Introduction

The artist—whether painter, composer, or writer—is an interpreter of reality. And that gives him great power, for he is also a *creator*, either for good or for bad.

What does he create? He presents us with an image of reality, but one that is necessarily subjective: it is *his* interpretation of reality. And there's the rub, as Shakespeare had Hamlet say.

The ultra-realistic paintings of, say, a Norman Rockwell, while seeming to represent reality, in truth only present what Mr. Rockwell wants us to see. In other words, it is his slant, his take, on what is reality, but as seen from his personal viewpoint.

The artist as creator wields immense power because he can give an interpretation of reality that drives us to action, or to reaction. An historical example is Soviet-era "art," pure propaganda in the service of the government that caused the masses to be exhorted to action (think increased farm productivity).

But the artist can also be softly subtle in his presenting of reality, weaving a fabric of illusionary truth. The creator can lead us naïvely down the pathway of illusion until we find ourselves face to face with a world we never imagined might exist, but one that does not correspond to our understanding of reality. It can leave us confused or worse, causing us to question the very nature of existence.

My belief of the role—the task if you will—of the artist-creator is to present an image of reality that corresponds to the ultimate Truth that exists around and within us. He is to interpret reality in such a way that it reinforces and affirms the True Reality, one that is not subject to personal interpretation or subjectivity. I believe that the artists whom we call "great" did exactly that: they presented a metaphorical image of Reality to us, either through the visual, written or, that most powerful of mediums, music.

The temptation that may face the artist is to be swayed by the voice that says, "Did God *really* say . . ." (Genesis 3:1). Being a creator is an awesome responsibility, because the artist can willfully misuse the power at his hands to call into being a dystopic world that presents an image that erodes, not one that builds up.

Whole Cloth is my attempt to present subjective reality as a construct of a larger Reality, a reflection of the True image. Through stories that create verbal illustrations, I want to create a window that lets us peer more clearly into the world of ultimate Reality.

The hallmark of ultimate Reality, of Truth, is redemption. My hope is that the reader will catch glimpses of this redemption through many of these stories, and through them will be drawn closer to the Author of Truth.

Whole Cloth . . . *noun*

1. complete fiction or fabrication

But in order to make you understand, to give you my life, I must tell you a story.
— Virginia Woolf

A Worthy Son

I have always wanted to be a soldier.

Some of my earliest memories from childhood are of the times I waited with anxious expectation for my father to arrive home, resplendent in his uniform of the Roman Imperial Army. The polished bronze breastplate would catch the setting sun's golden rays, making my father appear—from my idolizing boyhood perspective—to be chief among the many gods whom we honored in our house.

As with those who pursue with zeal their childhood dreams, mine came true. I, Gaius Marius Cassian, did wear the same uniform as my father; donned the same brass and leather breastplate; armed myself with the same blade and scabbard; put on the same glorious helmet of Caesar's army.

Now the same sun's golden rays reflect off the Aegean Sea below us, creating a brilliant burst of sparkling light that shimmers like a thousand diamonds on its azure surface. The glints catch the corner of my eye as I sit on the terrace watching my grandchildren play. I am an old man now, long years removed from the time when my father strode into our home like a triumphant god entering the heavens.

My grandchildren, Marius and Diana, often beg me to tell them of the "old days" when I fought along the Northern March. They delight in hearing stories of heroic clashes against Britannic barbarians. Their mother sends the children to me—scampering like two jostling bear cubs—when she wants a few moments of respite. They sit at my feet, captured by and enraptured with never-old tales of long-ago courage and glory.

I almost died there, back on the Northern March. That was when I was—looking backward through the lens of time—more a boy than a man. I recovered from my wounds, only to learn what it really means to die. But that is part of my

1

story, one I am glad to tell to all who come this way and stay at our house here in Ephesus, as you have, traveling from the ekklesia at Rome on your way eastward. So I bid you, please take your place there in the comfort of the shade, and I will tell you my tale.

My father, Octavio Marius Cassian, was a career army officer who rose in the ranks to become a primus pilus, a senior centurion in the Roman Army. He served in the 2nd Legion under General Vespasian—yes, he who later became emperor—in the invasion of Britannia in A.D. 43. Father served with valor and distinction, and that caused him to be noticed by his superiors. As I was to later understand when I entered the ranks of the army, those who serve with distinction are given opportunities by which to prove themselves, and thus advance their careers. This means they are often away from home—for an army should be in the field putting down rebellions of the newly-conquered, or fighting against the barbarians who threaten the borders of our empire—not enjoying the luxuries of soft pillows and comfortable sofas in Rome.

My mother was a kind woman, but she did not understand the desires and childish imaginations of a first-born son of a centurion. Mother was of noble birth and didn't involve herself in the upbringing of her children, beyond the necessary supervision of the nannies. She undertook to entertain the dignitaries who visited our home, which followed the occasions when my father returned triumphant from a campaign in the provinces.

Children were not permitted to be present at such functions, but I would lead my younger sister, Junia, by the hand through the shadows of the house, telling her under no circumstances to utter a sound. We would hide behind a large urn, or a bulky piece of furniture, so as to get a clear view of the gathering—often from a vantage point lying on our stomachs. Years later I found myself in a similar posture on the damp, ferny hillsides of cruel Britannia in the gathering gloom of evening, spying on an encampment of barbarians grouped around their smoking peat campfires. My thoughts then drifted back to the times I unknowingly apprenticed for warfare in my father's house.

One occasion in which we children were permitted to participate was the victory march down the via Princeps to the Forum after one of my father's many successful campaigns. All of Rome, or so it seemed to my bedazzled child's eyes, came out to view this grand spectacle. Our family was allowed to sit in the reviewing stand with the other officers' families and the nobile—the aristocracy—all seated in order of importance. I would stand and salute my father as he passed by, just as he had taught me. But I wondered if he saw his adoring son in the crowd. I wanted so much for him to look for me and smile, bestowing recognition on a worthy son whose only desire was to emulate his father.

Afterwards at our house, the servants would shoo us away from the adults. Our teacher, a Greek slave, would take us to a quiet room in back for lessons. How I wanted to stand next to my father among the guests, looking up at his stern and manly face as he recounted splendid stories of war.

Father knew how to command soldiers in the field, how to outwit a foe in battle by his superior strategy, but he didn't know how to relate to his son. His manner was harsh—perhaps not intentionally—with an attitude that demanded, above all, obedience and respect. This he had learned through rigorous military discipline. Our relationship was marked by formality, and above all, criticism on his part—intended, I later saw, to provoke me to greater efforts.

I often recruited Junia in the restaging of Father's latest campaign, but she was an unwilling and cowardly companion, complaining about having to wield the heavy wooden sword against make-believe foes. Sometimes I substituted our long-suffering teacher in her place. When Junia wasn't available (or she, in her girl-like fashion, would run to mother for protection), I waged my battles against the ferocious lions of the gladiator arena, represented by several of our domesticated dogs. They, also, proved unwilling—and unworthy—opponents to my role as an aspiring soldier.

In short, I was often lonely, wanting the masculine companionship of my father, but full of self-doubt about my abilities. Paradoxically, at the same time I was anxious to learn and to put myself to the test. Though Father was gone from home for long periods of time, he remained for me a daunting standard of achievement and courage, one to whom I constantly compared myself. You will doubtless guess that I always fell short of this standard, as we invariably do when we seek the approval of others.

One of our writers has said, "He who desires peace should prepare for war." I took this proverb as a directive from the gods, and endeavored to prepare myself for such a vocation. There was no question that I would follow in my father's footsteps; because of my mother's standing, and my father's distinguished military career, I was welcomed into the ranks of the Imperial Army as an officer.

I will pass over the time spent in the basics of training: of maneuvers in various parts of the Empire; of my assignment to the 4th Legion; the ardors of field life in the army. But let me speak specifically of our time in Brittania. Of course, as my father's son it seemed ordained that I should go to the field of his first triumphs. Our company was garrisoned in the northern part of that god-forsaken country, charged with dealing with the frequent incursions of the Scots and Picts—savage barbarians with long, wild hair.

A Worthy Son

I'll never forget the sight that greeted us when our troops first landed on the rocky shore of that heathen country: dense ranks of armed enemy stood a spear's length up from the stony beach. Between the ranks, women in black attire dashed like Furies—their hair disheveled—waving flaming brands. All around them their priests, the Druids, poured forth dreadful imprecations against us. I can tell you now that in spite of our training, we felt scared. Such was our welcome to Britannia.

And now I come to the part of the story that my grandchildren like best. We went out that day to deal with one of the local tribes that was causing disorder on the outskirts of their village. I took a squad and we marched in the direction of the settlement. We heard their sounds before we saw them. Sure enough, when they spotted us—a rough group they were—they charged toward us, yelping and screaming at the top of their lungs. I ordered our troop to draw up in ranks, but the heathens were on top of us before we had time to form a proper defensive position. I drew my sword and went after one who looked to be their leader, and quickly cut him down. There was noise and confusion all around us, a tumult of swearing and shouts in several languages.

I heard a voice cry out in warning: "Gaius!" I turned toward the sound and saw the blur of a rough-hewn sword coming down from above, only just missing my head. It hit, instead, full force on my right shoulder, staggering me to my knees. My armor absorbed the force of the blow, but the sword cut through the leather casing and I felt a sharp pain in my shoulder, followed immediately by a numbness in that arm. My sword clattered to the ground, I being helpless to grasp it. The barbarian lifted his implement again, bringing it full over his head. His face was contorted with rage: his eyes seemed small and dark, remarkably like those of a pig. I waited for the inevitable blow, and found myself thinking how my father would be disappointed in me. All of a sudden the man's mouth opened, as though to make a sound, but none came out. His eyes sprung wide in surprise, and the shaft of a Roman lance appeared through his chest, bright red with his blood. The barbarian's sword never descended, and the man fell off to the side, the quick work of my subaltern's skill.

As I knelt there, gasping for breath, the sky grew dark and thick; the sounds of battle faded, as though I were borne upward by an invisible chariot carrying me away from that place. My head dropped forward, and the last thing I remember seeing was the dark, damp earth of Britannia coming up to meet me. Then darkness.

I awoke to the sound of moaning. The sound seemed to come from far away, a constant, soft crying out. You can imagine how unsettling it was to slowly realize that this sound came from me. I perceived dark, shadowy shapes around me, and as my eyes came into focus, I saw my subaltern standing by my litter. I motioned for him to come near, and as he bent down, I thanked him for shouting out to me in battle, giving warning of the impending blow.

"But, Sir," he said, "it was not I who called you."

"Who was it then?" I asked him, my voice enfeebled from the injury.

"Sir, I heard no voice," he said. "Only the sounds of battle."

I was greatly weakened from the loss of blood, but quite fortunate to have the services of a Greek doctor who had been part of our expedition. He did the best he could with the few herbs and other remedies available to him, but it soon became clear—both to him, as well as to my superiors—that I was not going to recover in that damp, fetid land. The decision was made for me to return to Rome for a period of convalescence. Thus it was that I made the wearisome journey back to my native land in a litter, one among many disabled by war, returning home for healing and rest.

And in this state I finally arrived for a time of recuperation at my parents' home. Mother was, of course, concerned and solicitous, hovering over my couch as I lay in a haze for days on end. Father was away in the province of Asia, conducting inspections of our garrisons in that region. He had learned of my wounds by means of the Imperial courier; word came back of his desire for a speedy recovery and that I return to my duty assignment as soon as possible. I was instead reassigned to the Praetorian Guard.

Two months after my return to Rome I reported to centurion Tertius Livius Maximus at the Praetorian camp. He had served with my father in Britannia and knew me from my youth.

"I've got an easy assignment for you, Gaius," he said. "There's a Jewish prisoner recently arrived from Judea. He's a harmless old man, although something of a fanatic about his religion." He paused and scratched his cheek. "You'll be trading shifts with another soldier while the man's here under house arrest. I'll give you the night shift," he said with a wry smile. "Maybe you can get some rest while on duty".

And that was how I came to meet Paulus, from Tarsus, in the province of Cilicia.

His house was not far distant from our camp on the Caelian Hill in the north of the great city, so it was a pleasant walk, as well as therapeutic exercise, to make the journey there in the late afternoon. I had recovered much of my strength by this time, although I had not regained sufficient use of my right arm to merit a return to the field.

The sights and sounds of the city in which I had grown up surrounded me as I trudged down the familiar streets: the rumble of country carts going down the narrow cobbled lanes, bringing their produce to the markets; the jabber of jostling pedestrians; the distant roar of excited crowds in the Circus Maximus, signaling a chariot race or perhaps gladiatorial combat.

Rome has a certain smell—some would say a stench—which is unique to the city; one never quite gets used to it. I walked through streets where the houses were aligned in compacted rows, each one close up against the other, in an attempt to accommodate the large number of people who had immigrated not long ago to the capital.

I finally reached the house in question (it was the custom for prisoners in Rome on appeal to rent a domicile), a modest dwelling on a quiet street removed from the main thoroughfares. It had a small, but attractive, walled garden in the back where a person could stroll and think beneath the shade of its leafy trees.

When I entered the house I was not pleased with what I found. The guard I was replacing, a certain Cassius Dio, lounged on a sofa, while the man he was assigned to guard walked at liberty in the garden area. Several other people, talking in groups of two or three, accompanied the prisoner while he strolled in the back.

I was incensed to find a Roman soldier committing such a flagrant breach of discipline, and I let Cassius know this in no uncertain terms. He was shaken, and mumbled an excuse and apology, neither of which I would hear. After a warning that Centurion Livius would hear of this violation, I dismissed him to the Praetorian. Meanwhile, those inside had gathered around to witness our little drama. I saw the prisoner—he was the only person old enough to fit the description I had been given of Paulus—looking at me in a fixed manner, but I observed neither fright nor awe in his regard.

A Worthy Son

My initial impression of him was his short stature: he was small in height and his build was slight, but in proportion to his figure. Slightly bowed-legged, he was wiry and full of energy—even when sitting. I think the energy came mostly from his eyes: dark, piercing orbs that fastened onto you like a shaft of sunlight reflecting off water. They almost blinded you with their power.

Walking up to him I said, "Sir, I am duty bound to have you shackled to me. This is," I added, "in accordance with the laws of Rome, as you well know."

The prisoner nodded in assent. "While we are in Rome, we must certainly adhere to her laws," he said. This he spoke in a serious manner, and I did not hear a hint of mocking in his voice. "However," he continued, drawing out each word, "the law will never bring us the freedom we seek." He continued to regard me with a steady and serious gaze.

"The law," I countered, returning his gaze without flinching, "is what ensures our freedom. That is why I am here."

His smile was gentle as he extended his arm for me to attach the chain.

Later, when it was nearing the hour for supper, I offered to unchain him so that he could partake of the meal without restriction. After the berating I had given Cassius, I realized how hypocritical this might seem to the prisoner. But if Paulus took note of this, he neither said nor indicted anything to remark it.

"Gaius Marius Cassian," one of his companions asked me. "Will you join us for the meal?"

At first I hesitated, as I didn't want to appear too familiar with a group that I had just met. But upon reflection I accepted, for my hunger was greater than my pride. Taking my place with them around a low, broad wooden table in the main room, I began to eat from the plentiful bowls of food, but paused when I saw that no one else was partaking.

"Shall we give thanks to God for this food?" Paulus asked me, with a deferential smile. I was not used to such religious practices, but decided to allow them this custom, since this was their belief. Paulus bowed his head, lifted up his arms, and recited a prayer in a strange language (I learned afterwards it was Hebrew, his native tongue). Without a pause, he switched to Latin:

"We thank you, O Lord, for this, your provision for our bodies, as well as for our souls. Bless these elements, so that we can be strengthened to do Your service." He then paused, and added, "And bless all here who take of this nourishment. In Jesus' Name."

There was a mummer of "amens" from the assembled group. I had never before heard the person's name with which he closed the prayer, and thought it strange that Paulus had invoked it.

During the course of the meal, the prisoner watched me as I ate and then asked about the limited use of my arm. When I told him it was from a wound I received in battle, he leaned toward me. "I'd like to hear of your experience," he said. After I told him my story, Paulus was silent for a moment, and then asked me a question.

"What did you think of when you were about to receive the fatal blow?" He looked at me, his eyes deep with concentration.

"Only about how much it would hurt," I lied. I didn't want to tell him about my fears concerning my father's approval.

"And did you not worry about what would happen to you, and where you would spend the after-life?"

"If the god Mithras chose, I would be selected to dwell in the light, on the side of Good."

10

"And what assurance do you have that you would be in the light, if you had died?" His unwavering look pressed in on me.

"None other than what I have done for good, here in this life. None more than any of us can hope for."

The prisoner looked down at his bowl. "None other than this," he mused in a quiet voice.

After the meal we lounged in the large room, and Paulus addressed the group in a discourse about his religion, much of which I didn't understand. I put it down to Jewish mysticism and foreign religion. He kept referring to a person he called the Messiah, named "the Christ," in Greek. I had a hard time concentrating, and so I walked to the back of the house, into the darkness of the garden. The night was cool that time of year, but pleasant. A young man who had been with us at table followed me; he was tall and slender, and his appearance suggested an age barely beyond youth.

"Gaius, may I have a word with you?" he said.

"Speak," I replied, and turned to face him, while resting my back against one of the trees. The flickering lights from the house outlined his delicate profile.

"You know, of course, the prisoner, Paulus, is a Roman citizen?"

"I have been informed of that fact, yes."

"Excuse me, Gaius," the young man said. "Pardon my rudeness. I am Timotheus; I come from Lystra, in the province of Asia." When I made no comment, he continued.

"Paulus is a great man. He's been like a father to me. When you get to know him, you'll see how great he is."

"So then, am I to treat him differently than I would any other prisoner assigned me?"

Timotheus lowered his eyes to the ground. "No," he said. "I just want you to realize how much he means to all of us here."

Whole Cloth

My face remained impassive, but my heart felt a stab of pain when young Timotheus spoke of the prisoner as being like a father to him. I turned away and walked deeper into the darkness.

Thus began a pattern of life for me that continued day after day without interruption: the walk from the Praetorian to the small house with the garden in back; the time spent with the prisoner; the suppers shared around the broad table; the teachings by Paulus lasting long into the night; the times of quiet sleep passed in the calmness of the house.

Several weeks passed. One day I entered the house for my evening shift. After the threat I had made to Cassius Dio—I never did report him to Centurion Livius, as I thought a good scare was worth more value than whatever disciplinary action the centurion might mete out—I myself had become lenient in the use of the chain when we were inside the house.

After I relieved Cassius, the prisoner came up to me. "Will you walk in the garden with me, Gaius?" he asked. I assented and as we strolled inside the perimeter of the stone walls, Paulus told me a story.

"A man had two sons," he said. "The younger one asked his father, 'Give me my share of the estate.'" Paulus went on to say that after the younger son took his inheritance, he went off to a foreign land and spent his money on wild living. When his money was gone he could only find work of the most menial kind—tending a herd of swine. Paulus explained that in Jewish culture it was forbidden to be in the presence of—let alone eat—pigs. After a time had passed the son went home to ask forgiveness from his father. He knew that he couldn't expect to be reinstated as a son, so he thought to hire himself on as one of the workers on the family farm. As he trudged homeward, he rehearsed the speech he'd give his father: "I have sinned against heaven and against you. I am no longer worthy to be called your son; make me like one of your hired men." But when the father caught sight of him as the son was still in the distance, he came running to meet him. The father embraced the son and called for a celebration—the roasting of a prized calf.

Paulus stopped and turned toward me, his gaze intense. "What kind of father do you think he was, the man in my story?"

"Well," I said, "this could never happen. The son is a scoundrel and deserves to be punished. And the father is a fool."

Paulus was silent as we continued to walk. Finally he spoke.

"Yes, the father is a fool. The son has no right to expect anything from him but the harshest punishment." He stopped and put his hand on my arm, gazing directly into my eyes. "But that story is about God, the God of the universe whom I serve. That is what He is like, Gaius." Paulus was peering with intensity at me now. "All of us are the 'younger son' of the story: we are scoundrels—and worse—and deserve to be punished. But God, in His mercy, pardons us. He is not," he added, "like the father we grew up knowing."

My gaze broke with his when Paulus uttered these last words. I felt a sudden pang in my heart, as if a cold dagger had pierced it. I lowered my eyes to the ground.

I was dumbfounded at what Paulus had said. I could not imagine a father who would forgive his son for such a failure. We had stopped under the outstretched branches of a fragrant tree. The setting sun rode just above the neighboring housetops, casting long yellow rays of warmth around us.

"You see," Paulus continued. "I, too, know what it is like to have a demanding, strict father. I, too, know what it does to your heart when love is given only in measure of your performance."

Whole Cloth

We continued our walk, but said nothing further. I was lost in thought about this story, and what he had said about a demanding father who metes out love in consideration for his son's performance. I could not conceive of a God who would act toward me otherwise.

During supper I found myself in a mental stupor, a kind of daze. My thoughts tumbled around inside my head, each atop the other in a haphazard way, with no order or purpose to them. Memories of my father flooded back: I saw the majestic figure from my childhood, but also remembered the fear and dread I'd felt towards him. His love and approval was what I had sought all of these years, but I never believed I could merit them. I deserved only criticism and disapproval for my insufficient efforts.

Toward the end of the meal Paulus asked me to stay in the room for his nightly teaching. "It will address," he said, "some of what we talked about earlier this evening."

I nodded an assent, too weary in heart to move to another part of the house. In a short while people, most of them known to me from previous meetings, began to arrive. Among them was a stranger, a slender young woman with dark hair, whom I had not seen before. Her hair was arranged in tresses, but even so it hung down to her narrow waist. She took her place at the back of the room, and Paulus began to speak.

"My friends, the Law is a good thing, but we cannot possibly keep it." He paused while the effect of his statement sank in on the assembly. He continued to talk about the Law (Paulus had explained to me some days before what the Jewish law signified for the Hebrew people), that it was not based on faith. He cited several writings, Jewish scriptures unknown to me at the time. "But Christ," he continued, "has redeemed us from the Law!"

There were murmurings of assent from the crowd.

Paulus went on to explained how the Messiah's death on the cross ("hanging on the tree," was how he put it) took the penalty of God's curse, how He took that curse so that both Jews and gentiles—I realized that included me, as a non-Jew—might receive the promise of their patriarch, Abraham.

While Paulus spoke, a strange thing began to happen. My mind began to clear of its haze and confusion, and the prisoner's words started to penetrate—how else can I express it?—into what seemed to be the very core of my heart. I heard the words he spoke, and my inner being received them like cool water flowing in a desert land.

"So then the Law," Paul said, "was our paedagogus, our teacher, to lead us to Christ."

I suddenly had a clear picture of what Paulus was portraying. I remembered our long-suffering Greek teacher from my youth, how he walked us to the school where we were instructed in the education of the day. It was his job to ensure we made it safely to and from school. What Paulus was saying was that the Law—all of the good things I had done, or was trying to do in an attempt to win my father's approval—was intended by God to frustrate us, so that it would lead us to Himself.

"When we were all children," and here Paulus glanced my way, "we were in slavery to the elemental principles—the 'ABCs'—of this world. But," he gestured with his wiry arm stabbing the air above his head, "in the fullness of time, God sent His Son, Yeshua, born of a woman, born under the Law, in order that we might inherit the full rights as sons of God. Because we are sons, we can call Him Papa (here he used the Latin word for 'Daddy')."

Paulus continued on, but I had closed my eyes and lowered my head, oblivious of the rest of the people in the house. I felt a tight knot form in my chest. A series of images of my father, of our house, of me as a young man striving to excel in my studies—all played in succession through my mind. Silent tears flowed down my cheeks, but soon I was overcome by the inner emotion and began to sob. The tightness in my chest intensified; it felt like a solid mass inside me was choking my life away.

I then felt hands on my shoulders, and Paulus spoke close to my ear. "Gaius, receive the True Father of the universe! Let the Christ come into your heart."

Other hands touched me: my back, my shoulders, my head. Little by little I felt a warmth envelope me, like honey being poured over my head. I heard a murmur of voices praying in different languages, but Paulus' rose above the rest as he prayed in Hebrew. In my mind I saw a "picture"—how else can I describe it—of someone who resembled my father approach me, his hand held out in welcome and with a smile of approval on his face. Suddenly the hardness in my chest began to lighten, and then I felt it dissolve. It seemed to melt by the action of my tears. I continued to weep, but I now felt joy instead of bitter sadness.

I heard Paulus' voice again: "Formerly, Gaius, you did not know God; you were a slave to that which is, by nature, not god. But now you know God, and more important, you are known by God. It was He, Gaius, who called your name on the battlefield that day!"

I raised my head and opened my eyes. Paulus was smiling into my face. "Welcome," he said. "Welcome into the bonds of freedom."

He clasped my shoulders and I was surprised by his strong grip. I looked around; people were smiling; some were crying. I noticed that the dark-haired woman I had seen earlier was in the group gathered around me. I felt somehow glad, and not embarrassed, to be here. I felt welcomed by them, and accepted in a way I had never experienced before.

A Worthy Son

Afterwards, when Paulus' teaching was over, the young woman came up to me. "We are so happy for you," she said. Her eyes sparkled in the light of the oil lamps; they were as deep as the sea and dark as her hair. She appeared to be very young, but seemed at ease talking to a man who was a stranger to her. I learned that she had come from the city of Ephesus, in Asia, accompanying her father on this visit to see Paulus. She had known the teacher when he spent three years in her city, several years before his coming to Rome.

Well, you have surely guessed the ending of my story. Diana, the Jewish girl from Ephesus, became my wife. But this didn't happen until I had left the army—my arm never fully recovered—and I had returned to my home. Mother didn't understand my joining this "new religion," as she called it, and withdrew from me in discomfort into the activity of her social life. Father, when he returned home from his travels, was unhappy about my decision to leave the military. He wanted me to try harder to rehabilitate my arm and stay in the service of the Emperor. But I no longer needed his approval, although I did want his blessing, which he was unable to give at that time. But I was at peace with my decision.

Paulus was brought before the Emperor not long after I left the army, and was, of course, acquitted of the charges. I spent many hours with him before he left for the West—Hispania, as some said. He talked about the necessity of living a life of commitment to the Lord, which he likened to dying a death to oneself each day. Since that time I have often pondered his words.

I returned with Diana to the city of her birth, where we are today, and worked with her father in his trading company. We joined the ekklesia here, and I later became an assistant to Iohannes when he became Bishop, after his exile on Patmos. But that is another tale, for another time.

The Abba of Sawtooth Mountains

The old man emerged from the slow swirl of fog and mist, wreathed in fragments of clouds, an other-worldly figure with his left arm outstretched as if feeling his way down a dark tunnel, his head lowered to protect against the gusting wind and spits of rain hurled from the clouds. He moved with a shuffling gait, his body bent over to one side. You could tell that he must be aching somewhere: his movements were slow, methodical and thought-out.

His hat blended into the gray, as much from years of sweat and wear as from the enveloping mist. A dark blanket, without any decoration save for a tattered border of stained sateen, served as his outer garment. He led the mule by a woven black leather tether; an impossible-looking stack of canvas bags, wooden boxes, and odds and ends tilted at a precarious angle, defying gravity, straddled across the animal's back—all held in place by a crisscross of worn hemp rope winding around a wooden frame mounted on the overloaded donkey.

"Aging ain't what it's cracked up to be," he said as he shuffled up to the uneven wood porch of the store where I stood, sheltered from the elements by overhanging eaves. "Remember that, young man, next time you think about gettin' old."

He didn't look directly at me, but comfortably accepted my presence as he tied the mule's reins with measured movements over the gnarled wood pole that served as a hitching post. That done, the old man limped up the steps of the porch to where I stood and extended his right hand in greeting.

"How far did you come today, Robert?" I hoped, for his sake, he hadn't been out in the weather too long. Robert had various campsites, or "caches," as he called them, scattered in the mountains and on the nearby plateau. He had lived in these parts long enough to know the terrain as well as anyone, but I worried about his safety as winter approached.

"I come far enough," he said in a laconic tone. He paused to shake the water droplets off his battered hat, slapping it against the side of his leg. He looked at his mule, who waited patiently at the hitching stand, head down as if lost in dreams of a more pleasant time. Robert's dark eyes were set in a tanned, weathered face, accentuated by a bushy, almost snow-white, beard. At first glance he was an intimidating figure, like one of the Wild West heroes who had populated the black-and-white movie screens of my youth.

"I reckon I need to get Rose over to the stable where she can bed down and get her some dinner," he said. Then looking at no one in particular, added, "Might want to get me some place to bed down and eat, too."

"I'll walk over to the stable with you, if you don't mind the company," I said.

"That'd suit me just fine. But then," he paused for dramatic effect. "I don't know what old Rosie thinks about it." I detected the trace of a smile on Robert's face. "Can you stand to have Ed around for a while?" he asked the silent donkey.

Robert Garrison was a legend around here, a man without age. He was born about the time the Wright brothers' airplane flew, but before the automobile was mass-manufactured, electricity sang through overhead wires, or the first radio went on the air. He was an anachronism in the latter half of the Twentieth Century: a man who ignored, but was not ignorant of, materialism and progress.

Robert had been a fixture around here for so long that several generations had grown up either knowing him, or hearing about his adventures. I'm sure the stories got embroidered on as time went by, but even if half of what you heard was true, it inspired a lot of awe and respect for the old man.

Robert preferred to live the way he wanted, which was trekking through the wilderness of the Sawtooth Mountains, following the meandering course of the Salmon River. Some folks held to the rumor that Robert was immensely wealthy: he had discovered a mine in the remote mountains with a rich vein of silver that he kept hidden from the rest of the world. He was parlayed into a kind of *El Dorado* of these mountains, a larger-than-life figure. Personally, I didn't believe any of it, because I knew Robert.

Looking at him now, anyone could see that he wasn't wealthy—at least, not by human standards. Oh, he was a character all right, and somewhat anti-social; he wouldn't want to sit around with a group of tea-drinking folks in some formal living room in East Boise. No, he preferred to be tramping in the mountains that lay to the north of our little town, leading Rose in whatever direction suited him.

He untied the mule and we set off in the direction of the stable. I pulled up the hood of my windbreaker against the fine mist, falling like microscopic silver beads around us. The streets were deserted and muddy, but that didn't seem to bother the old man, and certainly not his donkey.

"You know," Robert said in my direction, keeping his head down to avoid the occasional spitting bursts of rain, "it gets so that after a while old Rose here is as good a companion for me as any human being." Without breaking stride, he glanced my way, then looked away again. "You probably find that pretty strange," he said with a trace of humor in his voice. He shook his head from side to side, as though he were about to tell an embarrassing experience in his life. "You know," he said, "donkeys can see angels. Sez so in the Bible."

I tried to think of a reply that would make sense, but since nothing came to mind, I kept quiet. If you didn't know him, Robert seemed to be an eccentric old man, someone who bordered on the mentally frail, or perhaps even the dangerous. But like I said, I knew Robert. I wasn't worried.

Earlier in his life—which is to say at a time when many of us weren't yet born—Robert started out in business working in a general store as a stocker and delivery boy. That's how he helped support his mother and three younger sisters. He learned the ropes of merchandising and eventually worked his way up to a management position. Then, when he figured the time was right, he bought his own little store. One thing led to another, and in time Robert became the head of a small but burgeoning chain of grocery stores.

He met a young woman, fell in love, and married. They had two children, a boy and a girl. Things were going well for their family, and they enjoyed life as it led them along its intended course of pleasure and predictability. Then World War Two came along, and everything changed. Their son, Robbie, enlisted in the Navy and was killed when his destroyer took a torpedo during one of the big battles in the Pacific.

As we slogged toward the stables I heard him talking to his donkey, murmuring commentaries about life—or was it about their present situation? I couldn't tell. I guess the old man got so used to conversing with his jenny that he wasn't aware when other people were around.

Robert's wife was never the same after the death of their son. She withdrew from family and friends, inconsolable. She gradually retreated into a deep, black hole of depression where no one could reach her, not even Robert. He coped by throwing himself into his work even harder, going from dawn till dusk. Their daughter went to college out of state and never returned back home, at least not for any length of time. She married a boy she'd met at school and they moved back East.

The suicide of his wife was the breaking point for Robert. Her death crystallized all of the pain, grief, and loss he had experienced in life. He had no answers, but lots of questions.

"When you get that low," he once told me, "a feller either gives up or he starts searching for some meaning in life." Robert tried to bury himself in his work as he had always done.

"But that didn't work," he said ruefully. "I always thought that a man's job was his highest calling. I found out different." About the time Robert hit his emotional bottom, something significant happened in his life.

"God found me," he said. "Or rather, I found God. He was never lost."

Robert had been a church-going man, but by his own admission it was mostly a tradition. Church was just another social club with its own list of rules: who was "in," and who was "out." It was simply something you did on Sunday morning. It meant getting dressed up and wearing a new suit and shined shoes, but usually only when it was convenient. However, this tradition hadn't an effect on Robert during the remainder of the week. It was, as Robert later told me, "pure and simple, dead religion."

I met him during this time in his life. My company had transferred me from Seattle to the town where Robert lived, and as a produce wholesaler, I got to know him. When we first met I could see that something was bothering him, and it didn't take long before I learned of his personal tragedy.

Over time I was able to share with him what God meant to me, how He had worked in my life—although I knew that I hadn't gone through the difficulties Robert had. We had lots of talks there in his office. I brought him some books to read that had been helpful to me: Chesterton, Lewis, Thomas à Kempis. He gladly read them, and asked for more. Robert was searching, and step-by-step he began to find answers.

We got to the stables and I helped Robert unload his gear from Rose's patient back. She seemed glad to be there, as far as I can read donkeys. McCann's stable was a second home for her whenever they came back to town.

"Let me walk you over to Millie's," I said after Rose was bedded down. Millie's was the local boarding house, and Robert always had a room waiting for him whenever he was in town.

"Thanks," he said. "I'd appreciate the company." After checking to make sure Rose was comfortable, we headed up the street toward the two-story rooming house. The descending mist enveloped us in the blackness, pinpoints of swirling moisture in a fitful wind, illuminated by an occasional street light. It produced an eerie halo effect over our heads as we walked along in the dark.

Robert's walk toward faith took place over time, more of a journey than an event. I can't say that there was one definable moment when he passed from doubt to faith. It was more like a sailboat that was effortlessly—but purposefully— gliding, nudged forward by a silent and unseen wind. Robert recognized this change, and rejoiced in the peace that fellowship with God brought into his life.

At my invitation he began going to church with our family. Robert always had questions for Dr. Albright after the sermon, and our pastor was patient in answering them, as well as pointing Robert in a direction that brought up a few more. He told Robert that he was welcome to visit the church's library as part of his quest for spiritual growth. It was there that he found the book about the Desert Fathers.

Robert was fascinated by these spiritual astronauts of antiquity who lived over 1700 years ago. They had sought a deeper relationship with God by drawing apart from the world in which they lived. The Desert Fathers believed that society was a sinking ship they had to abandon in order to save their lives. And abandon it they did. Starting around the turn of the century in A.D. 300, men—but later also women—left their homes and families in the towns and villages of the Middle East to go live in the desert. The first of these pilgrims, Anthony of Egypt, lived in total isolation for most of the year. Every six months or so, people from his village brought him bread and other supplies. Over time they began to notice something unusual: Anthony didn't seem to be getting older; in fact, he seemed to be getting younger during his self-imposed exile.

People also noticed that Anthony grew in wisdom—spiritual wisdom. Before long folks from miles around would make pilgrimages to sit at the feet of Anthony, or "Abba" (the Semitic word for "Father"), as they called him. As time went on, groups of people began to live out in the desert, away from the distracting and corrupting influence of society. And so the monastery movement was born.

I guess it was about six months after Robert started coming to our church that he called me on the phone one day. Wanted to see me at his office; could I come over? When I got there Robert told me about his proposal.

"I been thinking, Ed. I want you to consider coming to work for me." He leaned back in his large upholstered swivel chair and regarded me thoughtfully.

I must have looked surprised, but after a moment he continued.

"I need somebody I can trust to help me with the company. And I can trust you." His dark eyes were intent as he looked at me from under bushy eyebrows that were beginning to turn silver.

I told Robert that I needed a little time to think about his offer; he said he understood. By the time I left his office that day I already knew what I was going to do. But I wanted to run it by Dottie and the kids before I came to a definite decision. Of course, Dottie was thrilled and so were the kids. They had become friends with Robert since we started inviting him over for dinner most Sundays after church, and occasionally during the week.

"I just can't stand the thought of that poor old man," Dottie said, "sitting in that big house of his, all by himself and feeling lonely."

Looking back on it now, I really don't think Robert was all that lonely, although he gladly accepted our invitations. The kids quickly took to him, and he to them. I guess, in a way, our children filled that empty spot in his heart he had for his own son and daughter. But he was also becoming a disciplined—and avid—Bible reader, and this filled many of his waking hours.

Robert and I worked well together: my knowledge of the business from a theoretical standpoint complemented his practical understanding of how to run a large company, learned from his many years of apprenticeship in the grocery business.

"Look here, Ed," he said one day when we were working in his office on a project. "I like you as a friend. But this decision to take you on is based solely on business motives." I later learned this wasn't strictly true. But I told him that was fine with me. Nevertheless, our friendship and shared spiritual values were an asset in our team operation of his business.

I should have seen it coming, but I didn't. It wasn't but a year later when Robert dropped the bomb on me.

"How'd you like to take over the business?" he asked, with something between a twinkle and a sly grin playing on his face. We had finished dinner after Sunday church, and Dottie was busy cleaning up in the kitchen. "Just run it for me, Ed, that's all," he hastened to add. "I'll still be the president, but you'll do the day to day operation." He watched while my mouth hung open, staring at him like he'd just told me he was from another planet. I had the usual protests and arguments against the idea, but Robert wouldn't have any of it.

"You already do most of the work here," he said. "I'll be in the wings to help out if you need it. But from what I seen, you don't need a whole lot of my help anymore."

I might have guessed at what was coming next, and probably would have if I'd been listening to the Lord more closely. Robert wanted to spend more time pursuing his spiritual search, but he felt restricted by the business and a life that centered around running a company.

In the end we agreed, and that's when Robert began going out into the Sawtooth Wilderness area for day trips, which soon turned into overnight stays. He bought a tent, cooking equipment, and all the things a man needs for serious camping. Being in the office without Robert at my side made me nervous at first. But I soon learned that his business was like a well-built machine: it kept on running regardless of who was at the controls.

As time went on, Robert spent more time away from town. He decided to get a donkey; if he wanted to spend more time out there, he needed more supplies than he could carry alone. We talked about building a cabin, but Robert didn't want to be pinned down to one spot; he liked the freedom to move around when he wanted. That's how Rose—the first Rose—came into his life. There have been several Roses, and the present one is number three, I think.

So Robert started his trekking. Weeks turned into months, and before long he was replicating—in the 20th Century—Abba Anthony's spiritual journey in the 4th. Meanwhile, life went on pretty much as it always had for my family and me. Our kids grew up; we got older. They met their futures mates and got married; we became grandparents, and there was more family in our house over the holidays.

But Robert didn't seem to be aging like us. Oh sure, his face got more wrinkled and weather-beaten, and his movements were slower. But his mind was sharp, and seemed to become sharper with the passage of time. When he came in from the mountains there was a peace about him, a serenity that you couldn't help but notice. He didn't say a lot when he was around people—a habit acquired, I suppose, from being by himself so much of the time. When he did speak, I learned to keep my mouth shut and listen.

"When I was walking in the Wilderness meadows with Jesus," he said to me one time, "He told me that we'd all be thirty-three years old in heaven." Robert paused to let that sink in. "As you know, that was Jesus' age when He died. Turns out that your body is at the peak of its physical abilities then. After that," he gave me a sidelong glance with a chuckle, "it's all downhill."

Another time he told me that everything in the world is in a constant state of giving thanks. "You ever notice the trees, Ed? They're always lifting their arms up to God in praise. That's the secret," he said, looking straight at me. "Giving thanks to God all the time, for everything." He lowered his head and shook it gently. "I can't tell you how much I regret all those years I spent in bitterness and complaining."

Sometimes I'd find him sitting in his favorite chair with his eyes closed. At first I thought he was sleeping, that he had nodded off as old people tend to do. But he hadn't; he was awake, listening to something—or Someone—beyond that room. Robert had learned how to hear from God in a way few of us have. For him, it seemed as natural as breathing, something acquired through years of solitude and isolation.

I could see the lights of Millie's boarding house peering at us through the mist. We had passed most of our walk in silence, something I'd grown used to when I was with Robert. I learned to wait for him to speak first, rather than trying to make idle conversation.

"You know, Ed," he said. There was a long pause as we trudged on. Our boots made faint sucking sounds as we walked along the muddy street. "I've learned not to ask the Lord for things anymore. I figure He knows what I need better'n I do, so I usually try to listen to what He has to say to me before I open my mouth." Robert turned his head and looked inquisitively at me. "You know what I mean?"

"Sure, Robert," I replied. I thought a while, and said, "Seems to me that's in the Bible somewhere." I smiled at him.

We walked on for several moments before he resumed speaking. "But there's one thing I have asked Him. I don't want to become like one of those old codgers you see sitting in a chair on the front porch, rockin' away, with nothing to do but count the cars and people that pass by."

I didn't reply, because he had unknowingly voiced one of my greatest concerns. Dottie and I had often pondered how we could talk this old man into coming out from his mountain desert, and return to a "normal life" in town—a place where there'd be people to look after him if something happened to his health.

"Well, sir," Robert continued. "The good Lord hasn't seen fit to answer me on that one just yet."

We stomped our muddy boots on Millie's steps, and I guess that made enough racket for her to peer through the window, and then open up the front door for us.

"Well bless my soul!" she exclaimed. "Look who's here! Robert, come in, come in. Your room's all ready."

Once he was settled in his room, I said goodnight. "We'll see you tomorrow. Dottie's expecting you for dinner at one."

"I'll be there, Ed. Looking forward to seeing your kids and those beautiful grandkids again."

I walked back home under a silent sky. It had stopped raining and through occasional clearings I saw bright pinpoints of sapphire blue starlight sparkling in the blackness, playing hide-and-seek with the drifting clouds.

When he didn't show up the next day, I got worried and called over to Millie's. She told me that she hadn't seen him that morning. He must be sleeping late, and she didn't want to wake him. I decided to walk over and check on him, as he usually wasn't late for dinner. But he *was* getting older, I reminded myself.

Millie let me in, and I walked up to Robert's room on the second floor. I paused before knocking, and listened at the door. It was quiet. I knocked a couple of times, good loud raps, and called out his name. When there was no answer, I gently opened the door and let myself in.

Robert was lying on the floor, stretched out full length, his feet pointing in the direction of the little white porcelain sink on the wall next to his bed. His arms were by his side, as though he were at attention, waiting to pass in review. It took me several minutes to see the small amount of dried blood that had seeped out from under the back of his head. I gently said his name, but I knew he wouldn't respond.

I glanced around the room. All was tranquil. Sunlight streamed through the white lace-fringed curtains in the window; scores of dust motes floated up and down in shafts of gentle yellow-gold light. Everything was silent, both inside and outside the room. I eased down onto the side of the bed; the springs creaked with a grating complaint.

Robert's Bible was on the dresser, along with some personal items. A damp washcloth hung lop-sided on the edge of the sink. I looked down at Robert's still form. The sunlight played on his left hand, enveloping it with a soft, gauze-like quality from the pattern of the lace curtains. A doctor later explained that the blood came from a scalp wound when his head hit the floor. But since his heart had already stopped pumping, he didn't lose much blood. He had simply passed on while washing up before coming over to our house for dinner.

"Well, Robert," I finally said, "the Lord answered your heart's desire, old friend." I felt dampness well up in my eyes, and for several minutes I just let the tears flow. A part of me felt sad, but another part—and this is hard to explain, but it was the stronger part—felt grateful that his wish had been so gracefully granted.

As I watched the pattern of sunlight slowly lengthen on his body, a transformation seemed to take place. I could see that the form lying before me was only a shell—an outer covering—and not the person himself. This was no longer Robert, the man we had known and loved for so many years. The real Robert, the essential weight of him, had slipped out quietly and unnoticed, and finding himself unhindered and unfettered, had risen above Millie's housetop, above the eastern plateau, above the Sawtooth Mountains, and continued to rise higher and higher until he became surrounded and enveloped by an immeasurable and transcendent light, and himself became light.

My Grandpaw Kearns

My Grandpaw Kearns was the smartest man I know.

Now, I don't mean "smart," like he had a lot of book sense, or even school degrees. Grandpaw never even finished high school, but that didn't make him not smart. My Grandpaw knew a lot of things about cars, engines, bicycles and guns. He also knew the most of any man I ever met about the woods and hunting and all.

Grandpaw used to tell me stories about when he grew up in the backwoods of Macon County, "a long way from the nearest town." He also told me that his family was "as poor as the day is long." All of his brothers and sisters had to help their paw with the farm and their maw with the chores around the house. It was hard work for all of them, but they pitched in together because all they had was each other to depend upon.

"It was hard work, Billy," he'd say. "We didn't have a tractor, just a team of sorry-looking mules and an old plow that kept breaking when we tried to plant in the spring." Then Grandpaw would smile a little, so that the corners of his mouth turned up. "But we all loved one another, and that made the difference."

He was not a very impressive man, as far as looks go. Grandpaw was thin and sort of short. Heck, I was even taller than him by the time I turned 15. But he was strong, and he was quick. I guess working for the railroad made him that way.

He had real pale blue eyes, the kind that made you think there was something going on behind them if you could just look deep and long enough. His hair used to be sort of a light straw color; I know that from the photographs Mom had of him. By the time I really got to know him it was pretty much all white.

Grandpaw Kearns was Mom's dad; my own dad went to Vietnam when I was just three-years-old. I don't remember much about him, except for what I call "snapshot memories"—brief scenes of a tall, friendly man bending over to pick me up. I also remember him taking me for rides in his yellow Studebaker. Dad was in a place called Da Nang in Vietnam. I guess it was pretty bad there, because he never made it home.

Growing up without a dad, I spent a lot of time with my Grandpaw Kearns. He and Grandmaw used to live on a small place a couple of miles from us, but after dad didn't come back, they moved into our house so that they could help with Mom.

Grandpaw was always doing something interesting—like taking his truck engine apart, or going hunting for 'coons in the woods. My mom and baby sister would stay at the house with Grandmaw and talk, but me and Grandpaw would always be doing something together.

He didn't talk a lot unless he wanted something, like for you to hand him a tool. I'd be standing by his old truck, watching him fix something underneath it and he'd look at me with those light-blue eyes, then wink and smile. "Hand me that box wrench there, Billy," he'd say, nodding his head in the direction of the tool he wanted. Otherwise, he didn't say much. "Folks that talk a lot don't earn their way," he'd say. "All that yakking gets in the way of honest work." He told me that was in the Bible somewhere.

I liked going hunting with Grandpaw. Like I said, he knew the woods and animals more than anyone I ever knew. Right from the start he taught me what he called "respecting the gun."

"Now Billy," he'd say, "make sure no one gets between you and the business end of that rifle 'cept the rabbit." And "Make sure you always got the safety on when you aren't aiming at something."

Grandpaw never really talked about it, but he was in the Army during World War II. As a kid I remember exploring the rooms in my grandparents' house by myself on rainy days. One time, I found a small cardboard box in his bedroom closet; when I opened it, there was a bunch of medals with different colored ribbons on them. Later when I joined the Army, I found out that Grandpaw had been in the Battle of the Bulge at the end of the war.

He didn't talk much about his being in the war, and never about his combat experiences. I'd ask him sometimes, but he'd just pretend like he didn't hear me, or else he'd smile and say that it was a long time ago and he really couldn't remember. But when I was in the Army I looked up a couple of the citations for the medals they awarded him. It turns out that Grandpaw was one of the few Americans who had evaded capture by the Germans; he spent days in the forest by himself. I guess growing up here in the country helped him out back then.

I finally got my first rifle when I turned 16. It was a birthday present, but Grandpaw and I had talked about it for a long time before. We discussed what kind to get, what was the best make, and we read gun magazines to find out what the well-known hunters recommended.

I saved up a lot from the paper route, and Mom helped out some. I later learned that Grandpaw had given my mom some money, but he never told me that. We had to order it through the catalog because the town we lived in wasn't big enough to have a gun store or even a Western Auto. Grandpaw wanted me to get the gun with telescopic sights. He said it would be useful for hunting squirrels and such.

I remember the day it came. The post office called our house, so Grandpaw and me drove there to get it. We put that long, rectangular cardboard box in his truck—up front with us, not in the back—and then drove home. He helped me put it together and showed me how to put on the telescopic sights.

"They's like the sights on a gun I had once," he told me. I knew he was talking about when he was a soldier in the war. That afternoon, dinner seemed like it would never end, and I could hardly eat anything because I was so excited.

Afterward, me and Grandpaw went to the woods to zero in the sights. There was a special target just for that purpose printed on thick paper that came in the box. That afternoon was the most I ever heard Grandpaw talk. He showed me how to hold the rifle steady against an old tree stump, how to pace off the correct distance to the target (we tacked it on a big oak tree), and how to calibrate the telescopic sight so that it was real accurate.

Going hunting with Grandpaw—me carrying my own rifle as we trudged together through the silent woods in the early morning, the fog rising off the river in the distance— was probably the happiest time of my life back then. We were like a team, him showing me little tricks about spotting small animals or how to compensate for the wind when it was blowing. He made sure I always cleaned the gun afterward, just like he did his.

One morning in October we were out in the woods looking for whatever might turn up, when Grandpaw pointed to an old fallen tree lying half-covered in autumn leaves. "Let's sit a spell over there, Billy." He patted a spot next to him on the log for me to sit down.

We just sat there, not talking, looking out at the shadowy gray hillside across the valley where the rising sun hadn't reached yet. You could hear the birds calling to one another from time to time, but otherwise it was still. Finally, Grandpaw started speaking.

"Your daddy (his country accent made it sound like "diddy") was a fine man, Billy."

He didn't look at me directly, but moved his eyes sideways toward me without really turning his head, then he'd go back to staring at the woods. I just waited for what he'd say next.

"He always did what was right; he was an honest man."

Grandpaw paused for a minute, staring off into the trees, but he wasn't really looking at them, if you know what I mean.

"Your daddy answered our country's call when it came. He asked me to look after your momma and you kids till he came back."

He lingered in the silence for a minute.

"Shoot, I wanted to go with him, to look after him, show him the ropes. What did he know about war?"

Grandpaw kicked at the leaves with his foot in an impatient sort of gesture. "But they told me I was too old."

The birds had become silent, and we sat there for a while. I think that was the most emotion I ever heard Grandpaw express, especially about my dad. Since I really didn't remember much about my dad, I couldn't feel much in my heart about him, a man I never really knew. But sitting there on that log with Grandpaw, he was telling out the hurt that was in both of our hearts right then.

"Your daddy'd be right proud of you. Billy," he finally said. His voice sounded a little choked. I glanced over at Grandpaw, just in time to see his eyes glistening with moisture. But he blinked a few times, then slapped my leg.

"Let's get going," he said. We can't let them rabbits get the better of us, now can we?"

Whole Cloth

Grandpaw couldn't come to my graduation from Army Ranger training; that winter had been pretty rough on his health. But I made sure he got the portrait photo they took of me with my Ranger beret and special shoulder patch and all.

I called home when I finished Sharp Shooter's school several months later. I wanted Grandpaw to know that I had graduated at the head of my class. Mom was the one who told me that Grandpaw Kearns had passed away in his sleep the night before. I recall how the tears felt so hot when they sprung up in my eyes and how my throat seemed all choked and narrow when I tried to speak.

I felt real bad for a while. But later on when Mom said how they found the picture of me in my Ranger uniform under Grandpaw's big hands, lying right on top of his chest, the hurt eased. I think he already knew his grandson was going to be the best sharp shooter in the Army.

Fighting Dragons

Because the road was curving, he wasn't going all that fast when he came upon their car.

The narrow two-lane blacktop had led him along its meandering length that morning through the spring freshened rural countryside; tall dignified trees bordered each side of the road, their fresh green leaves just coming out from winter dormancy. According to the road map it was—appearances to the contrary—a state highway.

Their car was pulled off on the right-hand side of the road under the outstretched branches of a tree that was native to this region but foreign to him, listing heavily to the left, the rear fender settling down protectively over the flattened tire like a mother hen guarding her chicks. A Black family—a man, his wife, and several children of assorted sizes—were standing behind the car, looking at the tire in a helpless sort of way, as if wondering how this strange-looking object had come to be there.

Perhaps it was the fleeting glimpse he got of the man's expression of resigned helplessness behind the silver wire-rimmed glasses, as well as his body language—the stooped shoulders, head bowed slightly forward, as if acknowledging the inevitability of defeat—that got his attention, as well as his sympathy. But it was the man's clerical collar, a white circumference of starched rigidity encircling his light brown neck that cinched it for him. This was, after all, Sunday morning.

He pulled his red and white 1956 Corvette off to the side of the road ahead of their car, then put it in reverse and then drifted back, stopping just in front of the disabled car. He had bought the 'Vette back in college thinking it would help enhance his masculinity, but all it did was help deplete his checking account. He put on the emergency brake and then looked around him; there was no other traffic on the road that morning.

When he got out the family was still huddled in back of the listing car. The wife and children seemed to be using the man as a shield, as if this newly arrived stranger posed an uncertain, but hostile, threat. Pieces of a disassembled car jack were lying askew on the ground beside the tire.

So he asked them the obvious question: "Do you have a flat tire?"

Obvious, perhaps even stupid in retrospect, but it seemed important to establish a cause, a reason, for them being stranded on the side of this road in rural Mississippi on Sunday morning in May of 1963.

He had graduated from the university mid-term in January, then headed down to Florida for flight training. He was now an Ensign in the United States Navy, an officer and gentleman by act of Congress. Growing up out West he hadn't been around many Blacks. Hispanics, sure—the migrants from Baja California and Viejo Mexico—there were plenty of them around town, especially during the growing season.

At his university there had been some Blacks, but looking back, he couldn't recall seeing any in the multi-tiered dorm where he lived. Since he hadn't had much contact with them growing up, he thought he didn't have any prejudices about Black people—which meant that he hadn't the opportunity yet to develop any hatred toward them.

"There's a problem with the jack," the pastor said, spreading his hands out in a futile gesture. He was not a large man, his build was on the lean side, probably several inches below the Good Samaritan's 5-foot-10-inches. But there was a quiet dignity that he carried in his stature and demeanor, especially in his face. The eyes were attentive and contained a depth of intelligence that spoke of wisdom. His skin was the color of amber honey.

The Good Samaritan offered to take charge of the tire situation, and the family gratefully accepted. Growing up his father had taught him how to handle tools and this had given him some degree of confidence in things mechanical; he quickly figured out how the jack went together and soon had the car up off the ground.

The pastor answered his occasional questions gracefully: he was Chester Pullins and his wife was Amanda. That was Joshua (the tall one), Aaron (the smaller one), and twins Yolanda and Yvette. Chester was the pastor of several small rural churches, the largest of which had, on a good Sunday, maybe fifty people in the congregation. Chester made the journey between his churches in rotation every Sunday. The flat tire happened between two of them.

After he mounted the spare on the wheel, the man stood back and lit a cigarette. Belatedly, he felt a twinge of self-consciousness about smoking in front of the pastor, but it was too late now. Ignoring the cigarette, Chester smiled and put out his hand, thanking him profusely, with a sprinkling of "God bless you's" mixed throughout. In the middle of his sentence the man saw the pastor's eyes fix on something beyond him, then slowly lower to the ground. His voice trailed away.

He became aware of the throaty rumble of a car's exhaust behind him, and turned toward the sound. A large dark-blue Chevrolet sedan with the markings of the Mississippi State Highway Patrol was idling, at a standstill, in the middle of the road behind them. The sole occupant of the vehicle was a beefy state trooper wearing dark sunglasses; he had on a gray shirt with a dark necktie that matched the color of the car. A flat-brimmed trooper's hat rested on the seat beside him and his straw-colored hair was cut in a short crew cut. He was staring intently at them.

"Whatch'all doin' there?" he inquired in a tone that was neither helpful nor friendly.

The man looked at Chester and waited for him to answer. After all, this was his State they were in. But the pastor's eyes were fixed firmly on a space somewhere just in front of his feet. The man glanced around at the rest of the family; they were doing the same thing.

For whatever reason, he'd had an intuitive fear of authority figures—especially policemen—since childhood. He remembered taking the blame without hesitation when confronted by an adult for any untoward incident or unexplained accident that happened among his boyhood circle of friends.

He looked back at the patrol car, to the policeman whose gaze hadn't deviated from them one iota. He motioned to the offending tire, still lying in the dirt.

"They had a flat and I helped them change the tire." He was self-conscious of how northern his voice sounded. He felt that he was ready to admit guilt for whatever law he had unwittingly violated.

"Where y'all from?" the trooper asked, but his question was directed solely toward the man. His head turned slowly toward his Corvette and its Midwestern license plate.

"I'm in the Navy," he answered. "Going up to the base at Greenwood for flight training." Why did he feel like he had done something wrong? After all, he had performed an act of kindness for this local family, so what was the problem?

"Y'all need to change your license plate an' get Mississippi tags if you're goin' to be living here," he said evenly and without emotion.

The man then made two mistakes: one, of correcting the trooper; and two—as he learned years later when his family chose to live in the South—of not calling the trooper "Sir."

"No, that's not true," he said with an authority born of youthful ignorance. "Since I'm in the military, I can keep my original plates as long as I'm in flight training." He stared at the dark sunglasses. It was a contest of wills between the Law and the Defender of Our Country. He thought he detected a scowl forming on the trooper's face, but with the sunglasses, it was hard to tell. The trooper was silent.

Chester broke the tension. "We gotta be moving on now," he murmured. "The Lord bless ya," he added quietly as he gathered his little flock and shepherded them into the car. The man took his cue and put the flat in the trunk.

"I wanna see your license." The state trooper hadn't moved an inch. He was still looking at him. The man also noticed that the trooper had positioned his car in such a way that made it impossible for Chester and his family to get onto the road. They sat in the car, silent and submissive.

"Roger Stratford," the trooper read out loud, looking at the driver's license. He took a long time with the license, writing down some things on his clipboard. He finally handed it back to Roger with an air of disdain and indifference. Without looking at Roger he said, "If I was you I wouldn't stop on the side of the road again like that. You never know what kind of people (and he stressed the word *people*) you might be dealin' with." He put his car in gear and began slowly moving away.

"And y'all better check on getting valid license tags," he shot back. "You just might get into trouble over that." He turned and looked at Roger for a fleeting instant as he said this, then drove away.

Chester pulled out slowly on the highway after the patrol car had left, heading in the opposite direction. Roger caught a glimpse of youthful faces peering out the back window at him, apprehension written in their eyes. Roger walked back to his car, feeling shaken by what had just happened. The old emotions of having done something wrong welled up from inside his chest with a sickeningly familiar echo. But what, exactly, had he done to make him feel guilty, like a felon sneaking away from the scene of a crime?

As he drove further north the landscape changed from gently rolling hills to flat delta. This was the region where cotton used to grow in abundance. There were still random fields strewn with leftover evidence of last summer's crop: small tufts of dirty white cotton, discolored by winter rains and mud, were caught in the roots of withered plants where the winter winds had blown them. The highway began to lengthen into stretches of predictable lengths.

He was just settling into an early stage of highway hypnosis when he was jerked back to reality by the red and white flashing lights in his rearview mirror. The front of the state highway patrol car seemed only inches away from his rear bumper.

"Oh, no!" he shouted aloud. "What have I done now?"

Restraining an urge to floor the Corvette and flee—his car against the trooper's, his masculine status symbol against the policeman's—Roger slowed down and pulled over to the shoulder. The police car mirrored his moves and held its near-drafting position on his tail lights, the pulsating beacons mounted on the roof emitting their high-wattage red and white message, matching the beating of Roger's throbbing heart. He had a sudden eerie presentiment as he looked into the rear view mirror at the emerging figure of the highway patrolman. It was the beefy, crew cut tormentor from several miles back.

He was much larger than Roger had thought, based on his earlier chest-up-only view through the patrol car's driver's window. As the trooper unfolded himself from inside his car, he looked to be at least six-foot three, with an ex-football player's girth and weight to match. He straightened his trooper's hat squarely on his oversized head and walked purposely toward Roger, metal clipboard firmly held in his meaty hand.

Roger decided not to look at him, but instead stared straight ahead at the flat expanse of delta that filled his windshield. He could feel the trooper glaring at him from behind his dark sunglasses. Finally he spoke.

"Lemme see your driver's license and registration."

Reluctantly Roger produced them. The patrolman took his wallet and didn't give it back. The charge was speeding, improper vehicle registration, and invalid driver's license. That's how he ended up in the Wayne County jail in Eureka Springs on that Sunday morning.

The jail was housed in the county courthouse, a building that looked to be at least over a hundred years old, situated on the raised central square of this small slumbering town. Inside, the hallways were dark and gloomy, with a pronounced smell of mildew combined with wood rot. None of the lights were on.

They walked down the deserted hallway, Officer Beefy keeping a firm grip on his elbow. For whatever reason, the trooper hadn't handcuffed him. But Roger didn't entertain thoughts of trying to escape from this larger-than-life police officer. They turned down another shadowy corridor and finally arrived at a doorway. The sign hanging from the bracket fastened to the dirty wall above the doorway announced: "County Jail."

The trooper pushed Roger in front of him through the door. They entered a large room that had several lights suspended from the high ceiling. Behind a square wooden desk sat a man in a beige uniform. He was just the opposite of his captor: short and thin, he looked to be on the farther end of middle-aged. His dark hair was slicked back over his balding crown. He looked up as they entered.

"Hey, Sammy Lee," he said. "Whatcha got?" Roger's captor now had a name.

"Oh, we ourselves a Yankee nigger lover," the trooper said, eliding the words into a seamless slur. It took Roger a few moments to decipher what he had said. He was to learn later that any person from outside the South was, by definition, a Yankee. Those from the North were Damn Yankees.

The booking was shrouded in a haze of confusion and fear. Roger remembered filling out a form, but didn't recall if his fingerprints were taken. He had an out-of-body feeling, as though he were looking at what was happening from the outside, like a scene from a low-budget movie. He had to empty his pockets of all their belongings, and the trooper handed the jailer his wallet. Everything was put into a large manila envelope and filed in one of the desk drawers.

"You got one phone call, by law," the jailer said to Roger.

His mind spun in feeble circles, not able to fix on one object for stability. What was he supposed to do? Finally the thought of calling the military base surfaced.

"I'll call the Air Station at Greenwood," he said. Then he hesitated. "But I don't know what their number is." All of his feelings of bravado back on the highway had deflated and escaped like air from a leaky tire.

"He don't know the number!" the jailer crowed to Officer Beefy, a gleeful tone highlighting his exclamation. "Well, what we gonna do 'bout that?" It was not so much a question as a statement.

"Give 'em the phone directory," the trooper said in an unemotional moment of generosity. He still wore his sunglasses, so his hidden features looked non-committal.

Roger found the listing of the base, and dialed the Duty Officer's number. For a brief moment he felt a surge of fear well up in him when there was no answer after the first several rings. Maybe the Duty Officer was out of the office on Sunday, and he'd be stuck in this godforsaken place for days.

But the Duty Officer finally answered, and after Roger gave a brief summary of his predicament, told the arrestee that he'd contact the base commanding officer. In the meanwhile, stay put. As if he had a choice.

The diminutive jailer sorted through a drawer in his desk and came up with a set of keys on a metal ring. He escorted Roger through a door in the back of the room into the jail proper. It was another large, high-ceilinged room; the floor space had been divided into a set of six cells constructed out of flat, narrow strips of iron, three cells on each side of the room. There was no obstructing partition between them, giving the jailer visual access to each cell. At one time the bars had been painted a flat black, but now they were rusting and peeling like a bad case of sunburn.

The only other occupant of the jail was a large Black man who was lying on the cot in his cell, snoring fitfully. Roger was put in the cell adjacent to him, and the jailer, after dutifully locking the cell door, left. Roger overheard the jailer and Officer Beefy talking through the thin wooden door. There was occasional laughter, punctuated by words such as, "nigger lover," "Damn Yankee sonabitch," and other, more colorful, epitaphs. Roger heard the jailer remarking in his high-pitched voice: "This'll teach 'em a lesson!" or words to that effect.

All of a sudden he felt very lonely, very afraid, and very angry. He was mad at these idiots he had involuntarily run into, and mad at how they had such power and control over his life. He began plotting how he was going to get even with them: plans of revenge began forming in his agitated mind, accompanied by dramatic images of physical assaults on the jailer and Officer Beefy.

Roger sat on the edge of his cot, an iron-framed rectangle covered with a thin, ragged mattress, and brooded. Shards of emotions from childhood—fear, confusion, loneliness—came crowding into his heart, making him feel hopeless. Some time later—he wasn't sure when it was, he had lost track of time—the jailer entered the room with a metal tray that smelled like it had food on it.

Unlike the prison movies he'd seen growing up where the tray was pushed through a narrow slot in the door, the jailer unlocked his cell and came in. He didn't seem concerned about the possibility of Roger escaping. Setting the tray down on the end of his cot, the jailer nodded in the direction of his adjacent cellmate.

"You got any of them burr heads up there?" he asked Roger.

"What's that?" he replied, unconsciously squinting his eyes in an effort to make sense out of the thick delta drawl.

"You got any of them burr heads up where you come from?" he said again.

Roger's puzzled frown told the jailer that he still didn't understand what he was trying to say.

"Niggers. You got any of them niggers up there?"

Roger was perplexed about how to answer, and felt stunned by the hatred he heard in this man's voice. He had insulted an entire race of people so matter-of-factly.

"Yeah," Roger mumbled. "I guess we do have a few . . ." He let his sentence trail off.

"Well, let me tell you something," the jailer continued, gaining fervor with each sentence. "Down here they have a whole lot better schools than we do. They got better homes than a lot of us. Why, some of my best friends are niggers." He smiled in a broad grin as he stated this proudly, as if he should get an award for having Black friends.

"The only trouble is," he nodded in the direction of the adjacent cell and the sleeping Black man, "they cain't hold their likker."

This was a theme Roger was to hear often during his stay in the South: it was a kind of litany, an expiation for any guilt White folks might feel because of the way they treated the Blacks.

After sharing with Roger several more pithy expressions of Southern culture, the jailer left, and he was alone again. His jailhouse mate was still sleeping. Roger looked at the tray of food, but felt nauseated. For the hundredth time he asked himself what in the world was he doing here? The overwhelming feeling of powerlessness was making him feel weak and sick. He lay down on the meager cot and stared at the ceiling through the bars of his cage.

Sometime later the door to the outer room opened again. Roger must have been dozing, because the sound of footsteps seemed to be coming from far away, as in a dream. When he opened his eyes and gazed at the figures in the sickly yellow light, he saw the jailer and another man. At first he couldn't make out who the other person was, but gradually his eyes focused and he recognized Chester, the pastor whose flat tire he had changed earlier that day—or had it happened in another world? He felt like he was in a time warp.

"Hey, Bubba," the jailer yelled in the direction of the sleeping Black man. "Y'all got a visitor. Wake up!" He dragged his key ring against the metal bars of the cell, producing a deafening clanging noise. The sleeping man shot up from his cot and looked about him, disoriented.

"Okay preacher," the jailer said. "Y'all's got fifteen minutes. I'll be back when the time's up." With that, the short warden went out and closed the door.

Chester approached the cell of the Black inmate. "Well, Broth'r White, I sure was sorry to learn that you got arrested." He put out his hands to touch the other's arm. "I wanted you to know that your wife and kids are being looked after by the church, so don't you worry none about that." Chester paused and glanced toward Roger, then turned back to his parishioner. He was about to say something more when the pastor did a double take in his direction.

"Why Mr. Stratford! Whatever in the world are you doing in that cell?" His look of concern was genuine, and for once, Roger was at a loss for words. Chester left his bewildered parishioner standing at his cell bars and moved over to Roger's side.

"Well, to tell the truth," Roger said, "I really have no idea why I'm here, except . . . something isn't right." He then explained to the pastor what had happened since they had first met on the deserted winding road that morning, detailing the events of his subsequent run-in with Officer Beefy. When Roger came to the part about the hatred he'd encountered, and the burning hatred he felt toward both Sammy Lee and the jailer—as well as toward the kind of people they represented—Chester frowned.

"Hatred is an awful thing," he said. "Believe me, I know. It'll consume you if you let it." He paused and frowned again so that his dark forehead wrinkled. "Oh, yessir, I know, all right. Hatred can put you in a prison of its own."

Chester looked up and gazed into Roger's eyes with his dark brown ones. "Did'ja ever hear that saying, 'When you go out to fight dragons, be sure you don't become one in the process'?" Roger nodded his head in assent.

Chester glanced around the cell. "Those people who did this to you are in a jail, too—a jail of their own making. The best way to fight against the kind of hatred you've encountered is with forgiveness and truth. Let them use their hatred; you gotta use forgiveness. Don't ever be tempted to join them." He smiled a quick flash of encouragement in his direction, then turned back to Brother White for some final words of advice.

About eleven o'clock that night, the jailer came back into the room. Roger was still awake. When he opened the cell door, the jailer held it wide and stood outside.

"Y'all's free to go," he said. "The judge called and said to release you. You're s'poss'd to go directly to the base up there at Greenwood."

It turned out that the commanding officer of the base was a member of the same country club where Judge Gifford played his weekly round of golf. Roger was released on his own recognizance.

When he got to Greenwood his troubles were far from over. He had to appear before Captain Swain and explain why he was arrested, how the charges had been trumped up by trooper Sammy Lee. It took a while, but eventually all the charges were dropped, but his ego still felt bruised and violated. Roger wasn't sure that he would be as able to forgive his tormentors as pastor Chester would.

Roger stayed in touch with the pastor while he was going through training at Greenwood; the family had him over for dinner before he left Mississippi and moved on to the last phase of his flight training in Texas. It was at Chester's house that evening that Roger experienced the concept of forgiveness—for him, always a vague, ill-defined theological construct that didn't have much practical application in the "real world"—come alive.

"Let me tell you," Chester said, "about a time when somebody chose to forgive a person who really hurt them." While Amanda and the twin girls cleared the dishes from the table, he proceeded to tell Roger about a young couple that had just married and had moved to a city a state away from where they had both been raised. This couple was looking forward to starting a family, but decided to wait until they both had good enough jobs, so that they could afford to provide for the children they wanted. One day not long after moving to this new place, the wife was brutally raped while she was coming home from her job. The police said they couldn't find the attacker, even though several people had witnessed the crime.

Shortly after this, the wife discovered that she was pregnant; it was clear that the life she carried within her was the result of the rape. The young couple prayed about it and decided to keep the baby. So in due course the child was born, but it wasn't the biological offspring of the father.

In order to bring this baby into the world, the couple had to forgive the attacker, even though the wife had done nothing wrong. The couple knew that the Lord wanted them to have the baby, although it was conceived as a result of the most depraved kind of sin.

Chester paused in his story and looked at Roger. "The reason I'm telling you this is because that young couple were my parents; I was the child born to them from that attack on my mother." Roger felt a lump start to thicken in his throat, but he couldn't take his eyes off of the kindly Black pastor.

"And there's more," Chester said. "The attacker was a White man, and that's the reason I'm a light-skinned Black. Can you imagine the ridicule I took from other kids as a youngster growing up, and from grown people, too? They looked at my parents, then they looked at me, and they knew there was something wrong. I was too light-colored to be their child. So I grew up with the continuing effects of this one man's sin against my mother, even though neither she nor I had done anything wrong."

Chester looked intently at Roger, who felt as though he were riveted to his chair. "So I've had to forgive this unknown White man every day of my life. The alternative would be to live in hatred and bitterness; I tried that for a while, but saw it was going to eat me alive. My papa taught me that only forgiveness will set us free from any prison anyone might want to put us in—including ourselves. So one day I got before the Lord and told Him that this was the day I wanted to stop hating, but I'd need His help to do it."

A short time after that Roger left Greenwood for further training in Texas. He and Chester promised to keep in touch. It was while he was in Texas a couple of months later that Roger received an envelope in the mail from Chester. Inside was a newspaper clipping: the authorities in Mississippi had found the bodies of several missing civil rights workers from the North, one White and two Blacks. State trooper Sammy Lee Blaine, among others, had been indicted in the crime. It turned out that he had driven the bulldozer that dug, and later covered up, their graves.

Roger stayed in touch with Chester over the years; he hears from him mainly at Christmas time when they exchange cards and family news. Chester is still pastoring several small country churches in Mississippi. Roger got a degree in social work and eventually decided to move to a small town in Arkansas.

As he thought back to that time in his life and reflected on the stories of people he works with today in his case load, Roger remembered Chester telling him what he characterized as his "Road to Emmaus" experience the day he decided to stop hating. "Yessir," Chester had said, "the way out of the prison of hatred is through forgiveness."

The Boy Who Flew Too Close to the Sun

Every year around this time I get to feeling sad.

It's when the leaves start to turn from their dusty summer greens to the yellows, reds, and oranges of autumn. There's a kind of gray-tinged melancholy that silently calls out to me from somewhere deep inside. I'll sit for a long time, staring at the reflection of the October trees on the wind-scarred surface of the lake. The sadness, like a lead weight on a fishing line, pulls me down until it meets the deepening darkness below.

It was Darlene who put her finger on it. "Oh, Honey," she said, "it's Paulie. Every fall you go into this depression because of him."

I guess she's right, although I'd have never come up with that myself. It's hard to see when you're looking at yourself from the inside. Yes, it was October that he died, but that was so long ago, back when we were kids. So why would I still be feeling the effects of that?

Paulie was a special kid, right from the start. Oh, I know—everyone says that about their own family. But in this case it's true. Of course, he was real special to me, being my only kid brother. It was just Paulie and me, because Mom couldn't have any more children after him. He was born when we still lived in the city, before Dad bought the place out in the country—"the farm," as he called it.

Even as a little baby Paulie wasn't like other kids. What I mean is, he wouldn't fuss or hardly cry at all. He'd sit in the faded yellow armchair in the living room, all propped up with pillows from the sofa, and stare intently at things in the room. He liked the way the sun came through the windows, making bright sparkles on the glass, or forming miniature rainbows on the bookcase from the light coming through the fish bowl. He'd smile and wriggle his hands and feet like crazy, like he was applauding the show God was putting on for him. When I carried him around the house in my arms, sometimes he'd tilt his head back and look at me intently, like he was memorizing my face so that he'd never forget when he grew up.

He began to walk when he was eight months old; he'd already been crawling for several months. But one day he just stood up, swaying back and forth like one of those plastic toy clowns with a weighted base that don't tip over when you punch it. He gave me a big grin, like he was saying, "Hey, Pete, look at me!" But when I yelled for Mom to come see and Paulie heard her quick, frightened steps on the stairs, he plopped back on his diapered bottom. But the next day she did see him walk, and from then on there was no stopping him.

Here's another thing about Paulie: unlike most toddlers he didn't get into things just to make a mess. He wouldn't pull books off the shelves and leave them scattered on the floor, or knock over sacks of flour in the pantry just to see the white swirls spread on the linoleum floor. No, Paulie would toddle up to something and then stare at it for the longest time. Sometimes he'd pick up what he was looking at and examine it from every side, like he was trying to decipher a code.

I'll never forget the day we took him to the department store downtown. He was about a year and a-half by then and had been walking for some time, so he got around real good—all upright and confident. Mom wanted to buy me some new clothes for third grade, and Weinstock's had a sale going on. So Mom, Paulie, and me drove there in our little red and white Rambler. I held him in my arms; this was before car seats became law. Like always, Paulie was checking out everything we passed. He'd turn his head to follow what he saw, then he'd see something new, and he'd have to track that, so his head kept swiveling back and forth all the way downtown. I remember laughing, thinking that was so funny, but Paulie was real serious the whole time. It was like not missing a thing was his mission in life.

Weinstock's was big inside, high and spacious—they don't make stores like that anymore. At the time it seemed to me as big as the football field over at my school. In one corner they had what they called the Luncheon Pavilion, which I later learned was a fancy name for a dining area. On Wednesdays the Women's Club held their noon meetings there, and they had a pianist playing the store's big black concert grand. We could hear the music as soon as we came in the front door.

We headed over to the boys' section, which was right next to the Luncheon Pavilion, and Mom started looking through the shirts and trousers piled up on a long table they had in the middle of the aisle. I wandered over to the Boy Scout section to look at the neat knives and canteens behind the glass-fronted counter. I got real absorbed looking at the camping stuff, so it was a shock when I heard her scream. I looked up to see what had happened.

"Pete!" Mom yelled, "Where's Paulie? He's gone!"

She was frantically looking this way and that, trying to spot him. I took off running down the nearest aisle, going as fast as I could, looking for a pint-sized little kid in a blue denim jumper and a red baseball cap. I could still hear Mom yelling behind me, and by this time other people were starting to take notice.

"Paulie!" I yelled as I ran, looking up and down aisles, my heart pounding like I was at a school track meet. But no

Paulie. I cut in front of the Pavilion area, still looking down the aisles, when out of the corner of my eye I saw something. There, under the big black piano, was Paulie; his little head almost touched the bottom of the soundboard. His eyes were closed and the expression on his face was something I wish I had a photo of. I didn't know what the word, "ecstatic," meant back then—but that was it. He held his arms straight out from his body, like he was imitating a statue.

"Paulie!" I yelled, and ran over to the piano. The women around the luncheon tables all looked in my direction, but I didn't care. I swooped under the piano and grabbed Paulie in my arms. His eyes flew open all of a sudden, startled-like. When I picked him up he started crying, which was unusual for Paulie because—like I said—he didn't hardly cry at all. He wasn't doing it out of fright, but out of anger and indignation. He wanted to stay under the piano and be swept along by the waves of music, like a surfer in the ocean riding the waves. I didn't understand any of this back then; it wasn't till afterwards that we learned what Paulie was like.

We left the store in a scene: Mom frantic and crying with relief, Paulie kicking and screaming in my arms, and me feeling humiliated. I never wanted to go back to Weinstock's after that.

Another unusual thing about my brother was that he didn't start talking at the age when other kids were beginning to sound out words and string them together to make sentences. He just seemed content to observe, rather than comment on what he saw. I'm not saying that he didn't talk; he'd say things like, "Mama," and "Dada." But most often he'd just look at you with his piercing blue eyes.

It was Dad who figured it out.

"It's like Paulie has his own little world inside him," he said. "All of his thoughts and feelings are like an internal dynamo, giving him the energy to keep going."

"What do you mean?" I asked.

He shook his head and smiled ruefully. "It's like he's self-contained; he really doesn't need anything from other people."

The other strange thing happened when Paulie had just turned three. We'd moved out to the country several months before, and Mom was feeling lonely, not having close friends like when we lived in the city. I was liking the farm pretty much because Dad let me drive the tractor when we'd cut the weeds in the big field behind the house. I was ten by then, and he could trust me on the tractor after he'd ridden along for a while.

Mom learned about a ladies' Bridge club that met in the small town where we did our shopping. They met every two weeks, and Mom jumped at the chance to escape the isolation of the farmhouse. She had to take Paulie to the meetings, because he wasn't in school yet. They met at Mrs. Clancy's house, and she had an old upright piano in the living room where the ladies played cards.

On this particular day, Mrs. Clancy had put on a phonograph record of Beethoven's "Moonlight" Sonata to play as background music for their Bridge game. Mom and all the other ladies got so absorbed in their card game that they didn't pay too much attention to Paulie. The next thing they knew the record had finished playing, and suddenly they heard the "Moonlight" Sonata, note for note, coming from the old upright, just like a record. Paulie was sitting on the big stool at the keyboard, playing the music.

There was a lot of "ooh-ing" and "aah-ing" as the ladies stood around him. Funny thing was, Paulie had his eyes closed. He was playing by ear, moving his fingers over just the right keys to make the melody. He was the hit of the afternoon, and the ladies never got back to their Bridge game after that.

At dinner that evening Mom told Dad what happened at Mrs. Clancy's. "Pat," she said, "we've got to get a piano for Paulie." When Mom gets a certain look in her eye, and a certain tone in her voice, you know she is never going to change her mind.

So that's how we got a piano in our farmhouse. It was a second-hand one Dad bought from an older couple in town. Paulie sat at the piano bench every spare minute, playing away. Instead of racing toy cars, or playing in the yard with the dogs and chickens, Paulie played the piano. He also listened to records that Mom bought, or to the radio— whatever kind of music was playing. He liked slow, gentle music the best, the kind that touches your heart, making you feel warm all over.

Dad worried about Paulie; he didn't like him staying inside the house all the time. "Mary," he'd say to Mom, "it isn't natural. The boy needs to be outside, playing with kids his own age, or coming with me and Pete when we do the chores around the place."

After we got the piano I spent more time with Dad, and he let me do a lot of things around the farm. I remember lying in bed at night just before I fell asleep, listening to the muted voices of Mom and Dad drifting up from the kitchen. They were arguing about Paulie. I didn't like to hear their angry voices, especially when they quarreled over my brother. It wasn't his fault he was that way—he just liked to play the piano instead of playing outside.

But things stayed the same between Paulie and me. When the afternoon school bus dropped me off at the entrance to the farm, I'd trudge down the gravel road to the house and there'd be Paulie, waiting at the door. He'd be all excited to see me, and then I'd have to sit down and listen to what he had learned to play that day.

"Sih, sih," he'd say, pointing to the armchair. So I'd sit.

A lot of stuff was what he'd heard on records or on the radio. But as time went by he started playing his own music, things he made up himself. I don't know how he did it; I guess it came out of what was inside his head. Some of his music was so beautiful it made my chest ache. It was like when you're drifting off to sleep, the way you get during an afternoon nap where you're just barely aware of what's going on around you. Other times it seemed like I was sitting under a waterfall somewhere in the tropics—like pictures I'd seen in National Geographic magazines—with the sound of the piano cascading all around, showering me with sparkling joy.

I'd try to tell Paulie about school, what the teachers were like and things we studied. But he didn't seem much interested in that. Oh, he'd listen, all right, but all the time he'd be looking through my books, studying the pictures. He still wasn't talking a whole lot. Paulie seemed content to mostly listen.

That fall we got real busy working around the farm. Right after school I'd change clothes and go outside to work with Dad. We'd repair fences, or mow the brown summer grass, or just do other things needed to get ready for winter. We had to make some repairs to the red barn, a large weathered building that stood off to the side of the house. Dad had a tall ladder leaned against the side of the barn so that he could replace some rotten boards just under the roof.

On this particular day I got home from school and was in a hurry to change clothes so I could help Dad outside. Paulie was following me around the house like my shadow, tugging on my pants leg because he wanted to play his latest music for me.

"Sih, sih," he said. He tried to pull me to the armchair.

"No, Paulie," I said. "I don't have time right now. I've got to help Dad outside. Later."

I hated the look on his face—a sad, disappointed frown that distorted his usually happy features. Looking back on it now, I wish I'd stopped for the few minutes it would have taken to hear him play. But I didn't; I rushed outside, letting the screen door bang against the doorframe as I went.

Dad and I got busy on a project over by the chicken house, and we weren't aware of what was happening until we heard a loud, piercing scream coming from the direction of the house. It sent chills down my back when I heard her. It was Mom: she was screaming in a way that was different from when we had lost Paulie in the department store. We dropped our tools and started running towards the house, but Mom wasn't at the house, she was by the barn. A terrible sight awaited us there.

It's something that's burned forever in my mind. People say that memories fade with time, but that's not true: every detail is as clear today as when it happened. Paulie's body was lying at the foot of the ladder. We could see right away that something was awfully wrong. His legs were crumpled up underneath him and his head was bent in a totally different way from his body. We called the fire department, but when they came, they told us what we already knew. Paulie was dead.

Later on, when I was older, I learned about the Greek myth of Icarus, the boy with the wax wings who flew too close to the sun and plunged back to earth in a fatal trajectory. Paulie had wanted to be with us, Dad and me; he probably thought he could help us. I know it sounds crazy, but who knows how a little kid thinks?

So he climbed up the ladder because he'd seen Dad working there the day before. What really gets to me is the image I have in my mind of Paulie going up that ladder, rung by rung, all the while getting farther away from his safe world—that inner place where he was comfortable and, most of all, self-sufficient. As he climbed higher, Paulie entered a mysterious, unknown region: he got nearer our world, which for him was a strange and fearful place, somewhere he'd never been before. I can just picture him looking up, and realizing that he couldn't live there. So he fell.

I was eaten up by the thought of how I hadn't paid attention to Paulie when he wanted to play his music for me, how I didn't have time because I was in too big a hurry to be outside with Dad. If only I had stayed in that house, even for a few minutes, the accident would never have happened. That thought haunted me for years. I never told anyone about it; I kept it a secret until I met Darlene and we got married.

I guess that maybe one day it will all make sense, but right now it doesn't. Sometimes when I'm sitting here by the lake, feeling the gentle warmth from the pale October sun on my face, I can get quiet inside and not feel that awful guilt eating away at my heart.

I see myself coming through the screen door on that fateful day and Paulie is waiting there for me, all excited. He wants to play his latest music for me, "Sih, sih," he says, and I sit obediently in the chair by the piano. I lean back as he begins to play, letting the waves of refreshing, restful sounds wash over and into me, like ripples on the wind-blown lake. I sit there for a long time, just listening to his music, and finally a sense of peace covers me.

The Sacrifice

"Are we going to church tonight?"

Janice turned from the sink where she was peeling vegetables in preparation for their dinner that evening. She glanced at her husband, seated in the family room, TV remote in his hand, surfing through the channels. She stood there, waiting for him to answer her question.

"Who's preaching?" said Brad.

Wednesday night, and Brad Dalby was into his weekly game of trying to find a reason for not going to The Temple.

"No one. They're starting small groups after the summer break, remember? And guess what."

"What?"

"Pastor Firth wants us to be one of the small group leaders. He called earlier today, when you were at work. So we need to go."

Brad chewed his lower lip and his face took on a look of ill-disguised annoyance while he mulled over the obstacle that had just presented itself. He'd had plans to watch "American Talent" at eight o'clock. Was there any way he could wriggle out of going tonight?

He finally sighed. "Well," he said with as much pained resignation as he could put into it, "I guess we'd better go then."

Janice smiled and nodded her head.

"So what are we going to be doing this quarter in the groups?" He still hoped there might a possibility of getting out of it, assuming the subject matter wasn't to his liking.

"Pastor said he wants us to do a new study. It's about the cults," she answered.

The tall man walked with a casual stride along the office corridor, glancing into the rows of cubicles lined up on either side of him. Like a mathematical grid, he thought. Each cubicle functioned as an individual office space at this cutting-edge technology company. A low murmur of voices, intermingled with clicks and beeps from electronic devices, made up the background atmosphere: each person entering data, speaking on the telephone, or downloading information from the Internet.

He paused outside a cubicle midway down the corridor, and glanced with studied nonchalance at his watch, as if checking the time. With a quick movement he stepped through the opening and paused, running one hand through his thick dark hair in a nervous gesture. The woman working at the computer terminal glanced up as he entered, then pushed back her chair with a questioning look, mingled with apprehension.

"Hi, Ruth," the man said in a conversational tone of voice that sounded forced. "How are you coming with the project data?"

She stole a quick glance at him, then pushed a button on her keyboard that brought up a different screen. "Here's what I've got so far; the core elements are still downloading."

He nodded, then bent down to look closer at the screen. "Yes, I see now what you've got there. Um, interesting." The computer's artificial glow highlighted the sharp contours of his face, angular cheeks bracketing a thin nose. He reached up with one hand and placed it gently on her shoulder, then murmured in a voice so low only she could hear him.

"It's on for tonight. Eight o'clock. Are you still up for it?"

Ruth nodded, her eyes fixed on the screen, seeing but not seeing.

He reached into his pocket and pulled out a small folded piece of paper, no larger than a small coin. He placed it in the palm of Ruth's left hand, closing her fingers over it.

"Here's where we'll meet. Be there at eight o'clock with the child."

Straightening up, he spoke again, but in a voice meant to be overheard by anyone listening. "Good, that's just what we are looking for, Ruth. Let me know when you've got the matching Q-numbers, and we'll go on from there."

"All right, Mr. Moore," she said.

When he had left she passed a finger over her upper lip, wiping off the thin film of perspiration that had appeared during the last five minutes.

"Thanks to each of you who've taken the time to be here tonight."

Pastor Firth was a short man, but he exuded intensity. His light brown hair was beginning to thin on top, but he combed it so as to minimize the appearance of hair loss. Pastor Firth carried himself with poise, a confident sense of command, as he walked back and forth on the raised platform at The Temple. He'd been ministering here for six years now; he knew every person in his congregation well. That was his job—shepherd of the flock.

"Tonight," he continued, "we'll be starting up our small groups again. I hope you all had a good time off during the summer." Not really expecting a response, he gave a perfunctory smile, then looked out at the faces in the auditorium. He liked that word better than the old one, "sanctuary." Something stiff and stifling about that. It was one of the first things they'd changed when he came to The Temple.

"You're going to find our fall study series to be most interesting," he said. Many of the faces out there looked bored, disinterested. People seldom looked him in the eye when he spoke. It was always a challenge to keep his people on track; you had to have something with which to compete, given what was out in the media these days.

"We've found an excellent new book, one that's just been published by our headquarters press, and we'll be using it as our study guide." He reached over to the podium and held up a red-jacketed book. "Here it is: 'Know Your Enemy, a Guide to the Cults.' I've just finished reading it, and it's good. But scary. I want us all to read it. That's why I've selected it for our fall small group study."

Some of the faces were looking up at him now, glancing at the book in his hand. So many things to distract from what was really important. Worse, there were still spiritual forces around, even today, that could lead his people astray. And it was his job to make sure they knew what those dangers were.

Ruth turned the key in the lock with one hand, then held the apartment door open with her foot while she maneuvered the stroller across the threshold. The baby was still sleeping, his chubby face slumped over to one side on the blanket. He was a good baby, almost sleeping through the night now. Ruth's mother, a retired schoolteacher, kept the baby during the day now that Ruth had returned to work.

She looked up at the clock on the living room wall; Benji should be coming home any time now. They would eat dinner, then go the meeting. They'd already decided on it, but it hadn't been easy for her. There was so much fear she felt; it filled her heart every waking moment, ever since they'd decided to do it.

The Sacrifice

The baby stirred in the stroller, making a small cooing noise. Like a bird, Ruth thought. "Come here, little guy," she said, easing the awakening infant out of the straps of the stroller and into her arms. He was getting heavier each day. Ruth held the baby against her shoulder, close to her body. Benji would be home soon, then they'd go. Ruth worried whether they were doing the right thing.

She turned around at the sound of the key in the door. Benji came in, briefcase in one hand, the mail from the downstairs mailbox in the other. "Hi, honey," he said. Ruth loved the way his face lit up when he saw her at the end of the day. He walked over and gave her a hug, careful not to disturb the still-groggy baby in her arms.

"How was your day?" she asked. Sometimes Benji looked so tired when he got home from work. And tonight was a special strain on both of them.

"Oh, the usual grind," he said with a depreciating smile. "You know how Carter likes to push us to meet the quotas." He held his arms out for the baby, but Ruth shook her head, not ready to give him up yet. She wanted to hold him as long as she could, especially tonight. Everything was going to change after the meeting tonight.

She turned away, still holding the baby against one shoulder, and walked into the kitchen. "I'll have dinner in fifteen minutes, if you want to get ready. We have to leave at quarter after; I've got the instructions right here." She held out the folded piece of paper for Benji.

He unfolded the small square and studied the writing. It was in code, as usual. They had to be so careful these days; so many people were against them, now that the government had passed the New Laws.

Pastor Firth noticed more people looking up at him now. He spotted Janice and Brad Dalby in the audience. Good: he wanted them as group leaders. The Schulls were there, too, over in the corner. These were people who would follow directions. That was important. Pastor Firth strode back and forth on the platform, warming up to his subject now.

"The cults are alive and well in this country." He stopped and looked out at the audience, pausing for emphasis with the red book raised in his right hand, waving it like a signal flag with each phrase. "Make no mistake about it: they are alive, and they are dangerous!" He had them watching now. Sometimes you had to get fired up before they'd snap out of their lethargy and pay attention.

Pastor Firth stepped to the center of the platform, and looked with intensity at his audience. "Yes, I said, 'dangerous.' And I'm not exaggerating." He glanced at the book in his upraised hand.

"You're going to read, in this book, about one of the most pernicious, dangerous, and ungodly cults of all." He paused for effect, his dark brown eyes looking directly at the Dalbys. "Yes, right in this very city, there exists a branch of the cult you've all heard about. And it's true, everything you've read about them."

Pastor Firth took his time, looking from one person to another in the assembled group. "Human sacrifice." He heard the sharp intakes of breath, mostly from the women. "But sacrifice of the most despicable kind. They sacrifice *babies*." He lowered the book and held it out in front of him in a dramatic gesture.

"Yes, little babies, on their unholy altars. Then they drink the blood and eat its flesh." More gasps, louder this time.

Benji put his hand over Ruth's and patted it in what he hoped was a reassuring manner. "It's going to be all right, honey. Don't worry." He gazed into her eyes; he saw a lot of worry in them. Ruth was so sensitive, so intense in her feelings. She *felt* life—that's what drew him to her in the beginning. He glanced at the wall clock. "Look, you get the baby ready and I'll clear the table, okay?" He smiled at her, hoping to dispel her moodiness.

"Are you sure this is the right thing?" She gripped his hand with a new urgency. "I mean, we've talked with the priest and all, but . . ." Her voice trailed off and she stared at the top of their kitchen table, the soiled plates and glasses waiting to be taken to the sink.

"But what, honey?"

She paused, thinking, before she spoke again. "But what if they spot us going there? These New Laws are so frightening. I mean, what if we're caught? What we're doing is illegal!" Ruth gave him a frightened look.

"We've got to trust, Ruthie, we've got to trust." He glanced around the room, so homey and warm. Then he looked at the clock once more. "Look, Hon, we've got to be going. It's now or never. Are you ready?"

Ruth knew that Benji would never force her to do this. They both had a part in it. In the end each of them had come to the same decision. But still, now that the time was here, it was hard. She looked at the baby, playing with its hands, grasping them with jerky little motions as it lay in the small crib next to the table. So innocent.

Brad and Janice helped arrange a dozen chairs in a comfortable circle, then waited while people decided where to sit. Janice sat quietly and smiled, or at least tried to, glancing at the various people as the circle formed, while Brad helped them find a place to sit. She stole quick glances at the back of the book's red dust jacket, the part that described what the book was about.

After everyone found a place, Janice looked around and said in a semi-hushed, confidential tone of voice: "I can't *believe* that people would do this! I mean, sacrifice your own baby? I thought that sort of thing stopped in ancient times."

An older, dark-haired woman, who probably used hair coloring, took up the plaint. "Isn't that disgusting?" she said. "But I saw a TV program about baby sacrifice just the other day. It was a special on one of the cable networks. They say it really does happen these days."

"That's why the government passed that bill recently, making it a federal crime," a younger man with glasses said.

"Well, why in the world would anyone in their right mind do such a thing?" Doug Odoms ran an auto repair shop not far from where Brad and Janice lived. "We ought to drive those kinds of people right off the face of the earth!" He looked around, righteous indignation written on his face, looking for affirmation. Heads around the circle nodded in agreement.

Janice cleared her throat quietly, then opened the book to an early chapter. "Let's read a few pages in the book. It talks about the history of child sacrifice; maybe that'll help us understand what's going on nowadays."

Ruth and Benji took the bus to the midtown subway station. Ruth cradled the baby in a blue canvas sling arranged across her chest, one that freed both of her arms for carrying the cloth satchel that had baby's food and diaper changes. Benji felt the tenseness in her body as she pressed against him in the bus. He laid his hand on her knee, hoping his forced calmness would bleed into her. She stared out the window, silent. Every few minutes she breathed out a deep sigh.

"Here we are, Hon: this is our stop," he said. Benji bent over and picked up the baby's bag, then helped her out of the seat. They made their way to the exit door as the bus slid to a smooth stop. There weren't many people out tonight; he hoped that was a good sign.

The subway entrance was across the street. They waited without speaking at the stoplight. When the green walk symbol flashed on, they made their way across the intersection toward the brightly lit subway entrance. Ruth's face was drawn into lines of tautness, making her look years older. Fortunately the baby was asleep, pressed into the warmth of his mother's body.

They went down the entrance steps. Benji held onto Ruth's elbow, guiding her as he would an arthritic old woman, her steps hesitant and slow. When they reached the bottom, he looked around for the entrance to the platform, the one designated on the piece of paper. He could hear the distant deep rumble of an underground train approaching. Suddenly Ruth stiffened and stopped.

"I don't think I can go through with this," she said in a choked voice. Benji turned to face her; she was trembling noticeably under her dark topcoat. Her face was white, chalky like the station's walls.

"Honey, you can do this," he said. "I'll be with you each step of the way." Benji turned to look full in her face. Her eyes were unfocused, darting from side to side. "You can do this," he said, more emphatically this time. He smiled with what he hoped was both sympathy and encouragement. He grasped her hand, and with the other, gently stroked the sleeping infant's head through its blue wool cap. Ruthie always took care to protect the baby when they went outside.

She drew a sharp intake of breath, and pulled herself up a little. "All right," she said. Benji could see the taut muscles of her jaw working. "All right. Let's go."

Benji steered her toward the tunnel entrance, stopping at the kiosk to insert coins in the turnstile slot. Once through, they walked at a slow pace toward the platform. Ruth put a sheltering hand over the baby's head, as if to protect it from the increasing noise of the arriving train.

"Right here," Benji said to her, motioning to a large advertisement pasted on the wall. A policeman stood fifty feet down the platform facing their direction, his hand resting on a long black nightstick. Ruth shivered involuntarily.

"Just look casual," Benji told her, moving his mouth sideways like a bad Humphrey Bogart imitation. Glancing out of his peripheral vision, he saw the policeman begin walking toward them, looking straight in their direction. There was a sudden increase in the noise level, almost deafening in its intensity, as the approaching train emerged out of the tunnel. The ground vibrated in unison to the train's rhythm; the baby stirred fitfully against Ruth. A sharp gust of wind from the oncoming train pushed against them; they turned their heads away from the flying dust and scraps of paper swirling in the air.

The train came to a stop and its doors slid open with a pneumatic sigh. The policeman hesitated, then turned toward the open doors and entered the car next to them, glancing back over his shoulder at the couple with the baby standing at the edge of the platform. Benji and Ruth moved forward as if to board the train, then at the last minute stepped back to the platform.

The doors slid shut, and a moment later the train began moving out of the station in its onward journey, the sound of hissing air coming from somewhere underneath the cars like a deflating balloon. As the last car of the train disappeared into the black mouth of the tunnel, a transit authority worker came walking up the platform and then stood next to them.

He was a young man with a light brown mustache and eyes as pale blue as the early morning sky. He had on worn gray denim overalls and a clipboard in one hand. He casually drew a small symbol on the bottom of the worksheet and then tilted the board toward them so that they could see. Benji looked over at the penciled figure, then nodded, an almost imperceptible gesture. The worker turned and walked along the platform, away from the main entrance, toward the dark hole of the tunnel.

Ruth and Benji followed at a discreet distance. The worker stopped a few feet from of the end of the platform, now covered in shadow, away from the bright station lights. He pulled out a group of keys and selected one from the jangling cluster, then inserted it into the lock of a large black metal door recessed in the tunnel's wall. Ruth and Benji walked just beyond the door and stood looking back toward the station. When the worker opened the door, they quickly turned and stepped through it into darkness.

Pastor Firth looked around the empty auditorium. It had been a good meeting; introducing the book had gone well. The small groups were suitably outraged by the talk of child sacrifices, the baby slaughter. The Dalbys had led a spirited discussion group; most of the members had worked themselves up into righteous ire by the end of the evening. Future meetings would build on this energy, he was sure.

His aim was to show how, from the very beginning of the sect, child sacrifice—alluded to in a sort of metaphorical biblical language, tantalizingly vague, not clearly stated—was an accepted practice. And it continued to this day. He would show them all what it meant. His job, as Pastor Firth saw it, was to create in his people such an aversion toward this outlawed sect that none of his flock would ever be in danger of straying from the straight and narrow way.

"We've been literally driven underground, as you can see," the young transit worker said. Benji thought he detected a fleeting smile on the man's face as the door closed behind them. He held onto Ruth's arm, keeping her and the baby close.

"Just a minute, folks," the young man said. They heard the soft thudding of his boots going down metal steps, a dull metallic echo. Then silence. A heavy click, and a sudden illumination: weak yellow light drizzled from electric bulbs fixed into the ceiling. Benji saw a metal staircase that curved around to their left and then descended into the darkness below. Benji braced his hand on the wall and felt the cold mass of electric cables sheathed in black plastic. They were fastened to the walls, thick as Amazonian snakes, and followed the descent of the staircase to the lower level.

"Here, give me that," the young man said, holding out his hand for the baby's satchel. Benji passed it over, then put both of his hands on Ruthie's shoulders, both holding and guiding mother and baby down the stairs. Ruth's body felt rigid and stiff beneath her coat, like hardened cement.

"What's your name?" Benji said.

The transit worker glanced at them for a second, then looked away. "It's better if you don't know. It's safer all around that way."

He led them down the metal stairway until they reached the bottom. They stepped out into a wide concrete corridor. The walls on both sides, from floor to ceiling, were lined with black power cables, neatly layered two deep, and fastened with paint-thickened metal brackets. They walked for what seemed like long minutes, turning down dimly lit corridors that intersected like a maze. From time to time they heard a distant throbbing from somewhere above their heads, gradually building into the heavy muffled sounds of a passing train speeding toward the next station.

The young worker finally stopped in front of a wide gray metal door. He paused, ear cocked to the door, and looked up and down the dimly lit corridor. He rapped twice, waited, and rapped more three times in quick succession. Benji heard a deadbolt being withdrawn from the inside, and the door swung open.

An older woman stood before them. "Welcome," she said, extending her hand to Ruth and Benji. She peered closely at the stirring baby in the sling, then motioned them to come inside. A number of people—perhaps fifty—were in the room, seated in folding metal chairs arranged in rows. The space was lit by the same dull yellow light as in the corridors. Ruth thought it looked like fog had crept into the room, making it hard for her to see clearly. A soft whine from some distant machine enveloped the empty space, filling the room with an eerie sound.

The woman walked toward the front; Ruth and Benji followed behind her. A long metal table was centered in front of the chairs, a white linen tablecloth placed over it. Mr. Moore was behind the table, pouring a clear red liquid into an ornate metal goblet. A small plate the size of a saucer, covered with a white handkerchief, was beside the cup.

Mr. Moore smiled at Ruth and Benji, then turned around and picked up a large rectangular cream-colored piece of fabric. Like a sheet, but heavier. A circular area the size of a large melon had been cut out of the middle. Multicolored cotton embroidery ran around the edges in an intricate, colorful design. Mr. Moore held the sheet before him vertically, then slipped his head through the opening. A man standing to his side handed him a long band of cloth. It was embroidered in red patterns all along its length, the color of blood. He draped this around his neck so that the ends hung down in front, reaching to below his knees.

Mr. Moore held out his hands for the baby. The people in the folding chairs stood up, making a dissonant scraping sound on the cement floor. Benji helped Ruth slide the infant out of the canvas carrier, then together they gave the baby to the priest. She let out a muffled sob as they handed the baby over. Mr. Moore cradled him in the crook of one arm, and with the other hand he reached inside the robe, searching for something in his trouser pocket. He finally extracted a small glass vial and held it up before him. It was the color of light amber. Using the fingers of one hand, he uncorked the vial, then turned to face Ruth and Benji.

"Who names this child?" he asked.

"We do," Ruth and Benji said in unison.

"What name do you give him?" the priest said.

"Joshua Paul." They had decided on the name last week.

The priest raised the vial over the cradled baby and tilted it downward. As the drops of consecrated water fell gently across its forehead, trickling across the fine brown hairs of its brow, he intoned the ancient words, their rhythm echoing in a pattern passed down through the ages.

"Joshua Paul, I baptize you in the Name of the Father, the Son, and the Holy Spirit."

Mattie

Matt's a rescuer.

Blame it on his tender heart: dogs, birds, snakes—all sorts of animals—eventually find their way into our home. As he grew older he shifted his attention from the less exotic sorts of animals to girls; there seemed to be a lot of them who needed rescuing. He also brought home a cat. That's how we got Mattie, or should I say, that's how she got us.

"Hey Dad, look at this," Matt said with a sly smile, pulling a small white puff of fur out of the pocket of his fashionably frayed denim jacket. It was a tiny kitten, all white except for a little black face, and equipped with a voice box that emitted mews two octaves above middle C.

"I was hanging out over at Angie's when I heard this sound," he said. Angie was Matt's girlfriend of the moment. "When I looked outside, I saw him wandering around between the houses." Clearly an orphan in need of rescuing.

My reaction was immediate. "Oh, no! No way, son. Take it back."

We really didn't need a cat—not another cat—particularly at this time. We'd just buried Sneakers, our mongrel Siamese, after a nineteen-year love-hate relationship that had left us with a household of shredded upholstery. We weren't looking for another stealthy marauder who could take up where Sneakers had left off, leaving malodorous feline "gifts" cleverly hidden in dark corners of the house—only to be discovered several weeks after the event—as well as tattered armchairs and sofas in her wake. I suspect that cats must go to school somewhere to acquire these clandestine arts.

"Hey Dad, watch this," Matt said with a grin. He crouched down, lowering the kitten to the floor. It set off in a resolute manner across the family room, tiny ears pointed straight ahead, teetering from side to side as it explored the high pile of our carpet. I could only imagine that Mattie's ancestral genes were kicking in, making her believe that she was prowling through the elephant grass of East Africa in search of some hapless wildebeest.

Despite my protestations, this micro-cat soon became a constant presence in our house, and then in our hearts. Who can resist a tiny kitty that emits high-pitched mews with such wide-eyed innocence? But not wanting to be accused of catnapping, I did make Matt promise to return to his girlfriend-of-the-moment's neighborhood and ask people about a missing kitten. He did, and reported that there were not even "Missing Kitten" signs around the neighborhood. Apparently no one had lost this little cat.

Her coloring was distinctive, different from any cat I'd ever seen. She was, as I said, all white, with a sleek kind of fur that reminded me of velveteen. The exception was the jet black fur outlining her face like a mask; it put me in mind of a 17th century princess attending a masked ball at some rococo Venetian palazzo, her delicate hand holding a black masquerade covering in front of her face. In addition, all four of her tiny feet and the tip of her elegant tail looked as if they had been dipped in a can of black paint.

At first we dubbed her "Matty," in honor of our son. But before long we realized our gender mistake and modified her name to "Mattie." In spite of her breed's fierce reputation in the wilderness, she had the gentle female disposition of the best of these domesticated creatures. But there was something more, something that made Mattie unlike any cat we'd ever owned.

I first noticed it one day when Mattie wasn't prowling around the house in search of who knows what kind of prey, although anything larger than a medium sized cricket would have been a challenge for her. Instead, she was lying beside me on the floral-patterned couch, curled up a tiny ball of snowy white fur bearing the emblem of a black mask. Her tail was firmly tucked around her like a zipper sealing a package.

I was reading a book and I had set the radio in the next room to the classical music station, just loud enough to give me "background music" while I read. Suddenly Mattie raised her head, eyes wide open, and unwound from her curled-up position. She swiveled her head in the direction of the radio, ears turning like a radar antenna in search of incoming targets.

"What is it, Mattie?" I asked. "What do you see, little cat?" She seemed so intent on identifying something, body motionless, eyes pointed straight ahead. But I didn't see anything moving in our room or in the adjacent one, where the radio was perched atop a small desk. Mattie jumped off the couch in one fluid, seamless motion, extending her body to full kitten length, and ran to the next room. Now she had my attention, too.

"Mattie, what's going on? What do you see?" She was sitting into front of the radio, head raised, ears fully forward. She wasn't moving, but her attention was fixed on the radio before her, as though to not miss a note. Occasionally her two-tone tail would twitch in a kind of shake—like a baby rattler's warning—then sweep off to one side and lie there.

Mattie's' predecessor, Sneakers, had been fascinated with the television set as a young cat. One day she had jumped up on the arm of the beige couch, the one that was closest to the set, and stared at the images flickering on the screen. She would spend long minutes engrossed in whatever was on, particularly if the actors were animals: she was captivated by moving images of birds and squirrels. But Sneakers had never listened to the radio.

Curious, I got up from the couch and walked to the other room at a measured pace, watching Mattie the whole while. She was absolutely glued to her post, head uplifted, ears in alert mode, tail doing that rhythmical twitch. I looked at the wall behind the desk: nothing was moving, no insect climbing the yellow striped wallpaper, no swaying cobweb casting cat-attracting shadows. I crept up behind her, not wanting to break the strange spell by any sudden movements.

Then it was over as quick as it began. She turned from her position in front of the desk, looked up at me, squeaked out a small mew, then tottered back toward the couch and her napping place. I followed her into the other room, vaguely aware of the program announcer saying something about, " . . . that was the Sonata in F, by Italian composer Domenico Scarlatti, performed by the Consortium Antiqua."

I disregarded the radio for a moment and turned my attention to Mattie, who was busy grooming herself at the base of the couch. I bent down and looked at her; she looked up with her little black furry face and locked eyes with me. I swear that she was smiling, but I can't explain to you how I knew. After a few more seconds of eye contact, Mattie turned and jumped onto the flowered print cushion of the couch, turned around a couple of times as if following her own tail, then settled down to resume her nap.

I watched Mattie out of the corner of my eye the next couple of days to see if she'd repeat her curious behavior, but she didn't. She was all kitten—cavorting with the changing shadows cast on the rug by swaying leaves outside, or stalking imaginary beasts of prey, usually my stocking feet as I sat reading on the couch. Her teeth felt like tiny needles in my toes as they penetrated through the soft fabric.

Later that week I was at my habitual reading place, the floral-patterned couch in the family room. Mattie was in another part of the house, searching out new adventures. I could hear the soft padding of her feet as she made her way around the room, and the occasional muffled *thump* when she collided with a chair leg or side of a table.

The radio was on to the same station as before, my standard background music. Absorbed in my book, I wasn't paying much attention to either Mattie or what was playing on the radio. At some point I realized that I didn't hear Mattie's soft noises anymore. It was very quiet in the room next door.

Curious, I got up to see if she had fallen asleep, something that regularly happened in the short time since she'd joined our family. We would often discover her little body sprawled out beneath a living room chair, dead to the world after an energetic playtime. Like a little child, Mattie played hard, but didn't have much stamina at this point in her young life.

I didn't see her anywhere in the room. Then I happened to glance toward the adjacent room, where the radio was. There she was as before, sitting upright with lifted head, in absolute concentration on something in front of her. Her ears twitched occasionally; otherwise, the only movement was her tail—it flicked in time to some inner feline rhythm, little sweeps back and forth along the linoleum floor.

I watched her, fascinated. What was capturing her attention so fixedly? Then I became aware of the music playing on the radio. To my ears it sounded old: quaint, something from several centuries ago. All of a sudden I saw it. Her tail was keeping time with the beat of the music. No, it couldn't be. I looked again. Yes, her little tail was sweeping back and forth in exact time to the music.

Time foreshortened as I stood there, like I had entered a parallel universe or perhaps another dimension of reality. I stood watching to see if her tail sweeps were a fluke, just an occasional movement that I had misinterpreted as a musical rhythm. But no, Mattie was counting out an exact beat to the tempo of the music.

Then the piece ended, and so did Mattie's tail beats. I turned up the volume to catch the name of the piece they'd played. The announcer came on: "We've just heard Scarlatti's Concerto Grosso in C Major, played by . . ." There it was again: that name—Scarlatti. Of all the music that this station played, the only times Mattie had sat in rapt attention before the radio was when this particular composer's music was on.

What was going on? I picked up Mattie and brought her up to face level so that I could look straight into her amber eyes. She didn't resist, but turned on her purr box, making a sound like a tiny wooden ball rattling around in her small throat. She gazed with unwavering eyes into mine. There seemed to be a real intelligence shining out of those yellow eyes, trying to establish a connection with me.

"Mattie, why do you like that music?" I said, almost expecting an answer from this little kitten. "Hmm? What is it, Mattie?"

With a practiced deliberation she stared into my eyes, opened her mouth, and emitted two well-formed meows. Not the long and pleading kind, like when she was hungry or wanted attention. No, these were like she was trying to actually speak to me, to communicate a definite thought or statement. But what?

I kissed her little nose while she closed her eyes, then set her back down on the floor. She calmly teetered away toward the other room, flicking her little tail smartly like a drum majorette as she went. I watched her, lost in my own thoughts.

There was only one way to solve this strange affair. I followed after Mattie and scooped her up in my right hand as neatly as an eagle pouncing on an unsuspecting prey. She kicked and struggled a bit, then settled down to expressing her displeasure by gnawing on the fleshy part of my hand with her little needle teeth.

We walked into the living room, where the big stereo was. Still holding the squirming kitten in my hand, I sat down in front of the unit and opened the door where my CD collection was stored. I sorted through the disks until I found what I was looking for: Bach's "Well Tempered Clavier," a 17th century set of exercise pieces for piano. Using my left hand I unsnapped the CD jacket and inserted the disk into the CD player. I punched the "play" button.

I turned Mattie over in my hands as I squatted on the floor and tickled her furry underside. The elegant chords of sparkling piano music surrounded us like tiny icicles falling from the ceiling of an ice cave. Mattie kicked with her rear legs against my hands, biting ferociously with her teeth at the base of my thumb. If she were six months older I'd be bleeding by now; as it was, her violent assault on my hands merely tickled.

Bach's music poured out of the speakers, but Mattie didn't seem the least interested. She continued her attack on the Hand Creature as some of the most sublime passages Herr Johann had ever written poured forth from the speakers. I punched the "Stop" button and ejected the CD. Brahms was next, and I chose at random one of the several disks I had of his music. Meanwhile I put Mattie down on the floor and let her explore the neighborhood of the living room. Brahms's Second Piano Concerto played forth, but

Mattie wasn't interested at all; not so much as a tail twitch was paid to his music.

The same held true for all of the other albums I put on the stereo that morning: Puccini, Rachmaninov, Gershwin, Beethoven—even some window-rattling organ music by Widor didn't make Mattie turn her head in my direction. There was something that I was missing.

I walked back in the direction of my reading couch, my mind combing through every detail since Mattie had begun this mysterious behavior. She trailed after me, making a series of crouch-and-pounce attacks on imaginary victims in her path. I stopped short of the family room, the wisps of an idea forming in my mind. It was one of those "Aha!" moments people talk about: one minute my mind was blank, the next minute a thought had burst in, fully formed—like Venus rising out of the sea shell. Now I knew what I had to do.

I walked into the living room where we had an old set of the Encyclopedia Britannica ranged on the bookshelves, a fortuitous purchase from a neighborhood yard sale a few years back. I traced my finger along the dusty bindings until I came to the volume marked *Sarsaparilla-Sorcery*. In pulling it off the shelf I nearly dropped it on my foot. As someone said, "Words have weight," and this volume was heavy enough to put a crease in your trousers if you didn't have a steam iron handy. I lugged it back to the couch and started turning pages, looking for an entry on Mr. Scarlatti.

Mattie jumped up on the couch next to me, her head cocked to one side, watching with an expression of concentrated puzzlement that only a cat is capable of showing. I began paging from the back of the book, getting side-tracked for a moment by the "Scherzo" article, illustrated by a reproduction of part of the score to Beethoven's Seventh. My goodness, he wrote a lot of notes!

Time to move on. Let's see: *Sculpture* . . . *Scotland* . . . *Schelling* . . . *Scabies*—oops, too far. Ah, here it is: *Scarlatti, Domenico.* Italian composer, b. 1685, Naples; d. 1757 in Madrid. What was he doing in Spain, I wondered?

I felt little paws pressing on my pants legs. Glancing down, I could see Mattie awkwardly climbing the hills and valleys of my lap, maneuvering to get a better position in front of the open pages of the book. Why is it that cats always like to plop down in the middle of whatever you are doing at the moment?

Mattie was staring up at the page, her little head positioned directly in front of the short article on the composer. I craned my neck over her head to read the article. It was short, hardly more than a paragraph. Signor Scarlatti wrote several operas, traveled to England, taught at Rome, then finally ended up as court musician in Madrid. Well, no great revelations here.

Mattie shifted her position in my lap, turning her head so she could look up at me. "Mee-ow," she whispered, a quiet sigh that seemed full of meaning, If only I could interpret what it was she was trying to tell me. Her eyes bored into mine.

"What is it, little cat?" I asked, returning her gaze. Without taking her eyes off me, Mattie put out her right paw and placed it directly over the entry on Scarlatti, so that only the "Sc" and the "tti" of his name peeked out from under her foot. "Mee-ow." She mewed again in that quiet, plaintive voice of hers. I felt a prickling of the skin on the back of my neck, like someone had just traced their finger down its length.

"What about Scarlatti?" I said. I continued to look into her eyes, so expressive, trying to communicate something to me. "You like Scarlatti, is that it?" I felt silly, talking to a cat. I did a nervous glance around the room, afraid someone might overhear the strange dialogue going on between us.

"Mee-yiou." This time her cry was a little louder and definitely more positive in tone. It sounded to me for all the world like a "Yes." This was getting spooky.

"You're telling me that you like Scarlatti, right?

"Mee-yiou." Louder this time, more affirmative. We were still locked into each other's gaze, human to cat, trying to establish a communication bridge that would lead to . . . where? I could just see the headline: "The Cat Who Likes Scarlatti!" Sub-head: "Orphan kitten digs 17th century Italian composer." This was becoming too weird.

I closed the encyclopedia with a snap, and lifted Mattie off my lap. She gave a protesting squawk but I was the Alpha Cat, the one in charge. I returned the tome to the bookshelf, trying not to think about what had just happened between a small white kitten and a grown man reading an entry from the encyclopedia. Now I knew what the next step was.

The following day I drove to a store that sold—in addition to computers, audio equipment, refrigerators, washers and dryers— a range of CDs. Not a great collection in the classical section; I had to search past the Rock 'n Roll, Reggae, Rap, and Oldies before I spotted what my father used to call Good Music. Tucked away in that thin section there was a small sub-grouping labeled "Baroque." Surely, this might be fertile hunting ground for Signor Domenico.

There were exactly two CDs of Scarlatti's music: one was a collection of his concerti grossi and sonatas; the other had the improbable title, "The Best of Domenico Scarlatti," performed by a German orchestra I'd never heard of. A colorful portrait of Scarlatti dominated the cover of this CD. Little did I know that this album would hold the clue to the mystery I was seeking to solve. I paid for the CD and drove home, prepared for another experiment with Mattie.

After a tedious few minutes spent removing the plastic wrap that kept any molecule of air or the smallest bacterium from the disk, I found an unexpected bonus inside the plastic jewel case: the liner was full of notes about Scarlatti's music, plus a wonderful biographical rundown on the Italian master's life—much more information than I'd found in the encyclopedia.

Besides a sampling of his operas, concerti, and sonatas, one of the CD's tracks was the Fugue in G minor, better known to music lovers as "The Cat's Fugue." The story goes that Scarlatti's cat, Pulcinella—named after a fictional character who liked to dress up in a white suit with a black mask over his face and create havoc wherever he went — loved to prance about on her master's harpsichord keyboard. Domenico wrote down what he heard the cat "composing," and voila, the Fugue in G Minor.

Scarlatti's picture on the front of the liner notes showed a distinguished looking man with a long oval face framed in a white, powdered wig. He had on a frilly long-sleeved shirt that puffed out in lacey ornamentation at his collar and at the end of each sleeve. Over the shirt he wore a brilliant gold brocade coat, more like a long vest, with gold fabric-covered buttons down the front. Finally, a deep blue satin cutaway coat (with gold buttons running down the right side) topped off the outfit. Quite befitting for the maestro di musici to the court of Spain's King Ferdinand VI.

So Scarlatti had been a cat lover, even writing a piece of music for his cat. Or was it vice-versa? That was interesting trivia, but how did it connect with Mattie's behavior? We shall see, I thought to myself. I inserted the CD in the player, then looked around for Mattie. She was curled up in the living room on the rose-colored armchair, one of her several sleeping spots. Perfect! I fancied that this was going to be a purely scientific experiment, or perhaps pseudo-scientific would be more accurate. I had no intention of waking her; I'd simply put on the music and see what happened.

I cued up the CD to the starting track, making sure the volume wasn't too loud. The soft strains of a chamber orchestra flowed into the room. The harpsichord came in shortly thereafter with its characteristic tinny, sparkling sound. I stood back from the CD player and waited.

Mattie bolted into the room, headed for the source of the music. She was alert, but had that just-woke-up look cats have when they come out of a deep sleep. She padded up in front of the CD player and sat down, tail flicking behind her. She was intent—no, more than intent: totally focused is a better description—as she sat there, ears erect and head upraised. Then her tail began keeping time with the music, back and forth, back and forth, like a feline conductor directing the orchestra. She was enjoying listening to this music.

"All right, Mattie," I said. "Let's see how you like this one." I pushed the Pause button on the machine, and clicked the Advance button, forwarding to track number 6: the Fugue in G Minor—the Cat Fugue. My finger hovered over the Play button as I looked at Mattie. She was looking at me with a curious expression on her black-masked face: a mixture of wonder and impatience, as if to say, "What are you doing? Let's get on with it!" I pushed the Play button.

What happened next is very hard to describe. Not because I don't have words for it, but because I'm afraid of being misunderstood, or accused of trying to over-dramaticize the improbable. But let me assure you: I saw it happen with my own eyes, although what followed certainly stretches the boundaries of credulity.

As soon as the Fugue began playing, this little cat became a dancing, prancing, hopping, leaping creature. She was no more a cat than I am a doorpost. Mattie almost did a back flip in her exuberance. And she did it all in perfect beat with the music! I was watching an extraordinary . . . a supernatural . . . performance. But it wasn't a performance; it was natural. It was joie de vivre personified, if you can say that a cat is a person. It was . . . a ballet. Yes, a ballet, performed by a white cat with a black mask, whose name was Pulcin—

I stopped abruptly, thunderstruck by what I had just thought, and almost said. She was Mattie, not Pulcinella. Or was she? My mind, in most situations normal, rational and factual, started running in a strange, unaccustomed track. I was venturing into a place where "normal" people, living "normal" lives, don't go. I was on the slippery edge of rationality—that place which I had always defined and held on to as reality, as a ship holds to a compass heading. Was Mattie really Pulcinella, Domenico Scarlatti's cat?

My brain was on overload, so none of this made any sense right then. Like Scarlet O'Hara, I'd think about it tomorrow. The Fugue came to an end and I hit the Stop button on the CD player. I must have hit it too energetically, because the CD case—carelessly placed on the edge of the desk—fell off, clattering to the floor. Mattie jumped in surprise and retreated several steps, her regard full of suspicion at the wayward case.

I bent to pick it up, but halted with my fingers just short of the fallen case. It had landed face up, so that the portrait of Scarlatti was showing on the album's jacket. Mattie saw it about the same time, and ran over to where it lay. I paused, bent over, and watched Mattie. She stared at the picture, and then looked up at me.

"Mee-yiou." She was trying to tell me something. This time I was sure of it.

"What is it, Mattie? What do you want me to know . . . can you tell me?" Of course she couldn't, why did I even ask?

"Mee-yiou . . . mee-yiou." This time more insistent. She looked at the picture, then back at me, her eyes filled with meaning and intent.

It was scary, but I stepped out and took the risk. "You know him, don't you?"

"Mee-yiou!" I clearly heard the word, "Yes," in her reply. As if to emphasize her answer, she drew her front paws over and around the portrait on the liner notes in a slow and deliberate manner—all the time looking right at me.

"Okay, I believe you." Oh my, what now? Yes indeed, what now?

"Music time over, Mattie. Let's take a nap." She sat back on her haunches as I picked up the case from the floor, then shuffled out of the room in the direction of the floral-patterned couch. I joined her there; it was time to think.

What were the possibilities? The scariest one was that Mattie was Pulcinella, Scarlatti's cat, reappearing in a sort of reincarnation. Did cats reincarnate? For myself, I didn't believe in that stuff about reincarnation; that's fine for Indians and their sacred cows, but not for Italians and their cats.

So what was left? It took me awhile to come up with the answer, sitting there on the couch, my mind spinning as fast, if not faster, than the CD I'd just played. Mattie, as if to commiserate and lend me comfort, snuggled up against me and fell into a deep catnap.

The answer had to be the bloodline; Pulcinella's bloodline, that is. Cats have offspring—their descendents, so to speak. Although there was no record of it (I'm not aware of the existence of cat genealogies), it's not improbable that Mr. or Ms. Pulcinella found the love of their lives (all nine of them) in faraway Madrid and had offspring. Then their offspring had . . . well, you get the idea. It's like the Biblical genealogies: "Pulcinella begat Rudolfo; Rudolfo begat Pasquale; Pasquale begat Sophia . . . ."

So Mattie could be a direct descendent of the celebrated Pulcinella. She had to be. But how had this distinguished (if only by association to Signor Scarlatti) cat line managed to cross over to America? Aha—back to the Encyclopedia Britannica.

Volume six: "*Immigration, American*; 1750-1910." As it turns out, animals small enough to be considered pets were allowed to immigrate to the United States with their owners from abroad until the early 1920's. Imagine carrying a cat on the long transatlantic voyages of yesteryear. But fear about transmitted diseases didn't rear its ugly head until later on in the 20th century.

But don't ask me how all this came about; I can't really explain it. I'm not a rocket scientist (or any sort of scientist, for that matter), just a retired high school Civics teacher who likes cats and classical music. I figure it was the combination of intuitive love of music, and feline memory, that somehow got genetically implanted in Pulcinella's offspring . . . but there I go, trying to be a rocket scientist. All I know is that Mattie was somehow linked to a 17th century cat named Pulcinella, who loved to parade up and down on the harpsichord keyboard, and her owner—who just happened to be a musical genius—set onto paper the cat's musical paw strokes.

Mattie continued to grow as the months passed, and our kitten became a cat. She continued to take naps with me on the floral-patterned couch, listening—perhaps subliminally—

to classical music. Occasionally Mattie would wake up, look into my eyes, and put her paw on my leg. She'd draw her foot across my leg in small motions several times, all the while staring at me. I learned that this was her way of saying, "Put on the Scarlatti disk for me." Needless to say, she loved the Fugue in G Minor the most, and wouldn't let me turn off the player until she heard that track.

Then one day she left. Simply disappeared. We had let her out in the morning for her daily constitutional; she usually stayed in the backyard, exploring for chipmunks or any bird foolish enough to land near her. I was working on a letter to our oldest son, the one living in Virginia, so I'd lost track of time. When I glanced up at the clock, I stopped writing and got up to let Mattie back in the house. Except she wasn't at the back door. Neither was she in the back yard. I called for several minutes, then went out to look for her.

But she was gone. We asked the neighbors if they'd seen her that morning; no one had. Of course we put up flyers around the neighborhood and knocked on doors in the housing development next door to us, but nothing turned up. She'd disappeared as mysteriously as she'd appeared at Matt's girlfriend's house some months before.

I mourned her loss for quite a while. It's funny the way pets can ingratiate themselves into your heart. But one day I had a thought about Mattie: if she was descended from her ancient ancestor, Pulcinella of Madrid, wasn't it also necessary that Scarlatti's cat's bloodline should continue to procreate onward from her namesake, the Italian character invented sometime in the 17th century? What I'm saying is, if one day a small white kitten with a jet black facial mask appears on your doorstep, give me a call.

I have some CDs you'll need.

Christmas Story

She flinches involuntarily whenever she sees the car, or ones that looks like it. When the dark green Honda Accord passed in front of her at the stop sign last week, she couldn't contain her reaction. Startled at first, followed by anger—a deep seething rage that she finds impossible to ignore.

But she doesn't show it, any of it. Instead she concentrates on presenting a neutral face, emotionless. That's how she deals with the pain, keeps it inside where no one can see it. Sometimes not even herself. That's how she gets through the days: one at a time, just like they told her in the support group.

It takes time, they tell her, but it seems to her that she's been through enough pain to last a thousand lifetimes. Hearing other parents in the group tell their stories of loss and grief sometimes helps; usually it doesn't. It only reminds her that life isn't fair, and that makes her mad.

She told God that He could have her life, all of it. How long ago was that? In her mind's eye she sees a young girl, no more than twelve, kneeling in her room upstairs, elbows propped on the bed, earnest in prayer, giving herself without condition.

"I want to know You, God; I want to be able to hear from You."

People warned her that it was a dangerous prayer, but she wasn't worried; God is good and He wouldn't ever give her more than she could bear. But she isn't so sure about the good part or even the bearing part anymore.

Rob comes home about the same time each day. He's tired but tries not to show it; he's got to be strong for her. That's his role as husband, that's what everyone tells him. He's got to think about his wife and her needs now. Chrissy's gone, so they don't go there. They don't even get close.

"So, how's your day been?" he asks, but he really doesn't expect (or want) an honest answer.

"Fine," she lies and puts on a fake smile. She's tired too, but wants to be there for him.

They both discover that staying on the surface is the safest place to be. They tried going deeper, but ended up in despair, or sometimes unexpected anger toward each other, toward God, toward Chrissy. So now they just pretend; it's easier that way.

The call comes in the evening. It's been dark for a while now that fall is coming, but Helen is still trying to adjust to the change of season as well as the time change. Fall back. She's missing the gentle dusk of summer, the prolonged fading of the light.

Helen is relaxing after cleaning up dinner; Rob's in the den, watching the game on TV, so Helen answers the phone. An official sounding voice asks her if she is the mother of Chrissy, and without knowing exactly why her heart seems to rise in her throat, even before he gives her the news.

She stands there, unable to say anything to the policeman, her mind frozen in some place that has no time, no beginning or end. She hears the words, but is unable to make sense of them: it's like he is speaking a language unknown to her. She wants to remain hidden forever in this place without time; that way she won't have to go where she dreads going.

"No, that dress is too small for you." Chrissy doesn't understand and is ready to throw a fit. They told her that girls were easier, that they were malleable, would want to please their mother. But not Chrissy: headstrong and determined, it seems that she and her mother have been in a contest of wills since day one. Even her birth was difficult; that should have given her a clue of what lay ahead.

"Here, try it on, Honey. See how it's too tight?" But Chrissy is determined to make it fit and doesn't listen to Helen. "It's not too tight," she whines, unable to bend over in the taut fabric, a stuffed sausage.

"I can't tell her a thing," she complains to Rob, who just smiles. She's daddy's little girl and knows, even at age four, how to bend him around her little finger.

Will this ever get better, Helen wonders to herself?

Helen sees her everywhere, always unexpected, heart-stopping. The girl two people ahead of her in line at the bank turns around and Helen can't breathe. Her hair is just like Chrissy's and the shape of her face makes Helen do a double take. She's not looking for her daughter, but Chrissy shows up when Helen least expects it and the effect on her is always the same: her heart does a funny kind of skip and her mind goes blank, unable to process this false reality.

And then afterwards the emptiness creeps in, followed by irreconcilable sadness. What does she think is going to happen—that Chrissy will come back, or maybe wasn't really even gone, a mistake on everyone's part? How she wishes her daughter would come back; she has something she needs to say to her.

The worst part is right after it happens, the shocked look on people's faces when they hear the news, the way they look at her and Rob when they run into them at church or in stores around town, like they had just stepped out of an alien spacecraft. Some of the people stand aside and then turn to point them out to their friends.

The second worst part is what people say to them: "Oh, I'm sooo sorry," with a sooo genuine imitation of concern in their voices, like a bad TV commercial. Some of them look her in the eye, peering like they were trying to see if she is suitably sad. "She was a special girl, you know."

Yes, we know, believe me, we know, but does saying it make the pain go away? Or how about: "God wanted her for an angel in heaven." So what kind of god would take a daughter from her parents just so He could have an extra member of the celestial choir, a fill-in, if needed?

At the funeral Helen determines not to cry in front of people; she hates people who spew out their grief, letting it splash onto innocent bystanders. It's like they are just seeking attention: "Hey, look at me."

She doesn't want to be looked at, so she learns how to close it all up inside, not let it out. Rob isn't as successful and cries easily when the pastor talks about Chrissy and the memories they all share of her being in Youth Group, at Sunday School, in the Easter pageant. Helen has to fight against the anger she feels toward Rob for betraying her in front of all these people.

As the days after the funeral go by the attention gets mercifully less, as though people think now that the mourning period is officially over she and Rob should just snap back, trust in God and carry on with life. So she plays along with the crowd and tries to fit back in, to be the way it was before. But it will never be the same. Never.

Helen tries to remember the good times with Chrissy, but all that comes up are the memories of the bad times, the times of mother-daughter conflict and disagreement. It's like her life is only a series of frustrations and anger toward Chrissy, and that makes her feel guilty. She flounders in the guilt, swallowing mouthfuls of blame and shame. Surely they had some good times; where are they?

It's a movie that plays continuously in her mind: her daughter's angry red face pressed against an invisible wall inches away from her, the raised tone of voice, almost shouting. Fortunately, mercifully, Helen can't remember the words, just the feelings. And the feelings make her sorrowful, the time wasted in anger and bitterness, instead of enjoying the daughter that God has given her.

Then comes a slow, creeping depression, born of self-condemnation and guilt. Is this from God, is He trying to get her to confess her sins, repent from her anger and bitterness? That thought makes it hard for Helen to function, to live one day at a time. It breaks down her impassiveness in the face of loss and reduces her to a silent, gray mood. The depression grows darker and people start to notice.

Her friend Sara is one of the few who have the courage to speak up. "Helen, I'm worried about you. What's wrong? Maybe you need to talk with someone, a person who can help you through this time."

Sara means well, but Helen doesn't want to see anyone, talk with someone who is paid to "help her through" the darkness. Her life settles into a uniform monotony of dark-gray; at least the incriminating memories of her battles with Chrissy fade into quietness, a blessing she thinks.

Helen watches with a young mother's pride as her little daughter teeters unsteadily toward her. Sitting on the couch, enjoying a rare cup of her favorite coffee—a brief respite from the 24/7 duties of shepherding this energetic bundle of look-alikeness—she can almost convince herself that it's been worth it: the uncounted sleepless nights; doing nursing duty; rocking a colicky baby; walking long miles up and down hallways.

Helen sets down her cup on the end table and holds out her arms to Chrissy, an invitation for her precious daughter to be swooped up in her arms, an intimate moment between mother and child. Instead Chrissy veers toward the shiny porcelain cup, attracted by the glittery gold stripe that encircles the rim.

"No!" says Helen, perhaps a bit too loud. Chrissy keeps coming, so Helen tries a protracted "Noooo," a stern face with pointing finger for emphasis. Too late Helen recognizes that the child is bent on seizing the cup, and Chrissy's unexpected burst of speed toward the attractive object is faster than Helen's reaction time.

"No!" Helen screams, but it's too late and the cup and its contents of liquid amber splash onto the pristine beige carpet. Chrissy stumbles, the cup tumbles, and she steps on the expensive cup, one of a set of six given to Helen by her mother. There is a finality in the splintery cracking as her daughter's foot reduces the molded porcelain to shards.

Helen cringes with shame now as she remembers the impulsive energy sweeping unbidden through her body; it causes her to reach back and slap her daughter with adult strength, sending the child reeling onto the carpet, adding one more object to the littered debris.

She and Rob stand on the rustic wooden balcony of the lodge, the incredible vastness of the mountains and forest sparkling in the sun, spread out before them like a scene from a movie.

He has his arms around her and she can't imagine being any happier than she is right now. God is fulfilling her dreams in a way she hasn't dared imagine: getting married; being a newly-wed; both of them wanting to start a family; growing old with their children, then grandchildren, all milling about them in happy confusion. It almost seems, as she stands on the rough-hewn planks, that it's too good to be true.

The Sheriff's Office report is tucked away in the left-hand drawer of her desk at home. The account is sterile and devoid of emotion, just like her. At 7:36 PM on October 14th, a 2013 Dodge Ram pickup ran a red light at the intersection of highway 17 and Wayland Avenue, impacting a dark green 2007 Honda Accord on the driver's side ("T-boning" was the way the sergeant from the Sheriff's Office explains it to Rob and her when he comes to their house that night).

The Honda was halfway through the intersection when it was struck by the pickup. Measurements made at the scene, combined with eyewitness's reports, conclude that the driver of the Dodge Ram was traveling at a speed in excess of 65 mph.

The Coroner's report concludes that death to the occupant of the green Honda was instantaneous.

Their pastor is the one who tells them about the Parents' Support Group. Rob thinks it's a good idea, something that they need, he says. But Helen isn't so sure; she wants to stay in her dark cocoon of silent grief and secret anger. In the end she agrees to go, to "try it out," an asterisked escape clause if she finds the group too intrusive, a threat to her guarded heart.

The group meets in the basement of a fraternal men's organization, white cinderblock walls decorated with black and white photos of elderly men posing in front of a banner at their regional conference ten years ago. Metal folding chairs with splotches of missing paint are arranged in a circle by the leaders of the group; coffee is made on the out of date brewing machines owned by the lodge.

The first time they go she feels awkward and embarrassed, a stranger among other strangers. The fact that they all share a common bond doesn't register in her mind; she's not ready to admit that someone else could have experienced what she is going through. Generalizing the tragedy to include other parents seems to border on the blasphemous to Helen.

She sits quietly, tuning out the conversation and comments of the other "survivors," as they call themselves. Not me, she thinks; I'm not a survivor because I wasn't in that car with Chrissy. She thinks about how she will get through today, and then the next day.

Helen doesn't tell Rob at first; she doesn't want to be wrong about it and raise false hopes in him, as well as in her. The feelings seem like the onset of the flu, but not so pronounced, a constant low-level nausea she's never experienced before. Maybe her period's just a little late. She wants to go to her doctor, but opts instead for a drugstore pregnancy kit. The brochure inside the package tells her that the results are not completely accurate and to check with her physician to confirm what the test shows: she's positive for pregnancy.

She feels excited and cautious, all at the same time. This is another installment in her life-long dream: having wonderful, loving, well-behaved children, an added plus on top of her fulfilling marriage to Rob. Life is good; God is good. Is there anything that can possibly make her happier?

Helen doesn't want to go back to the parents' group, but Rob has already made some friends there. He's Mr. Gregarious, a natural salesman and encourages her to continue coming with him.

"Remember how they said to give it five or six meetings before deciding?" he reminds her.

Helen figures that she can practice tuning out during the meetings and not participate in the discussions; she'll leave that to Rob. That way the time will pass more quickly. She tells herself that she's thinking like an inmate in jail, but it's true.

The third time they go there's a guest speaker. Helen comes out of her self-induced fog long enough to register that the woman speaking has just touched something inside her. She's not just mouthing platitudes, like so many of the people who come to the group.

After the talk and the ending affirmations (said by everyone in unison, holding hands in a circle, just like Girl Scout camp) Helen walks up to Janet, embarrassed like a schoolgirl approaching a teacher. She doesn't know what to say, but Janet seems to know what she's come for, doing an internal scan of Helen with her kind, perceptive eyes. Helen stammers around but ends up asking for one of Janet's cards and thinks about calling her for an appointment in a few days.

The contractions begin just as she's getting ready for bed. Rob times them, always the stickler for precision, the one who reads the instructions of any product before opening the package. Helen calls the doctor and he says he'll meet them at the hospital.

Helen hopes it'll go quickly, but once in her room at the hospital, the contractions slow down and then almost disappear. She's uncomfortable, and sorry that Rob has to camp out in her room, losing sleep along with her. Finally she feels the sharp, tightening pains begin again, and they go on for what seem like hours. The nurse measures her from time to time, but she's not dilating enough for them to get serious about things.

The hours stretch on and Helen is getting really tired. Rob is there at her side to encourage her, but she just wants it to be over.

"Having a baby is not that much fun," she says to him, weary and conscious of the dark circles under her eyes.

At last she dilates to the proper size and they're on their way to the delivery room. Rob gets dropped off before they push through the big pneumatic doors that go whoosh and seal them off from the rest of the hospital.

"Keep pushing," the nurse coaches her, but it hurts; whenever is this baby going to come out? She pants between contractions like they practiced in the classes for pregnant mothers, and then just when she is about to give up there's one last contraction and she obeys the nurse's encouragement and bears down with all the strength left in her body.

"It's a girl," the doctor announces matter-of-factly and then Helen is peering down at this beautiful red wrinkled face half-hidden in the soft cotton blanket nestled alongside her. Oh my God, she thinks, she's so beautiful and the pain of the last thirty-six hours disappears like fog evaporating off a lake. Another installment of her dream comes true and Helen knows that she is blessed.

She didn't want Chrissy to have a car; she's too young, she tells Rob. But all of Chrissy's friends have one and after all, she had Driver's Ed at school and has her driver's license. She *is* sixteen and a-half, as her daughter regularly points out to her. Rob takes their daughter's side and together they talk Helen into agreeing. Two against one, not fair.

They shop around the car dealerships for a used car, looking for something nice and reasonable. They end up finding the Honda through a want ad in the paper. It's in good shape, well maintained (important for Rob), and Chrissy says she'll get a job at the fast food place over on Cleveland, one mile from their home, to help pay for insurance.

"I don't think I'm ready for this part of life," she confides to Rob as they lead their daughter home, following behind them in what is now her very own car. "She's so young and driving is so dangerous." Rob, as usual, discounts her fears and Chrissy is happy.

"Thanks, Mom," she says and gives Helen a hug, surprising her. She hangs on to the memory of her daughter's smile, putting it into the slim mental scrapbook that commemorates the times when she and Chrissy were at peace with one another.

Helen feels nervous and clumsy when Janet comes into the reception area to escort her back to the counseling room. Helen vowed that she'd never do this sort of thing, paying a professional to listen to her, but here she is and it's too late to back out.

Janet is easy and it's not long before Helen feels like she's just getting together with an old friend to chat about things. Janet knows how to start the conversation and she steers their talking from Helen's growing up years and her marriage to Rob, to Chrissy without Helen being that aware of it.

Janet doesn't push and Helen adds one more thing to the list of what she likes about her. She wants to tell Janet about her anger toward so many things: Chrissy; Rob; people; and now God. She wants to tell her that she feels like He's betrayed her, promised one thing, but tricked her into giving up far more than she would ever have agreed to if she'd known.

But Helen doesn't go there. It's too early in the relationship and she's afraid of Janet's reaction, even though she knows there's no real basis for that fear. Maybe later, she thinks. Janet looks at her and casually says, "Our time is up for today. Do you think you'd like to come again so we can talk some more?"

This is the chance for Helen to say that she needs to think about it, which is really a way to gracefully leave and never come back, to stay protected, remain safe. But she surprises herself when she replies that, yes, she'd like to return and meet again with Janet. The counselor takes out her appointment book, consults it for a moment, then looks up at Helen with a smile that makes her look ten years younger and says, "Well then, how about sometime next week?"

Helen feels that she has no more time to herself these days. Between making bottles for Chrissy, doing dirty diapers, feeding her daughter, changing her, trying to keep up with cleaning the mess she makes just in doing the ordinary chores a mother of a newborn has to do, there's not an extra minute left over for her, for relaxing, for sitting quietly and assessing her life up to now.

Instead it's constant activity from the time she's awakened by her daughter's cries coming from the crib set up in their bedroom, to when she finally puts Chrissy down at night. Helen is too exhausted to carry on a normal conversation with Rob. This is the new normal, she thinks. What a fool she was to think that she'd be able to have the life she'd imagined, like in the pages of some woman's magazine: a radiant young mother with perfectly coiffed hair and immaculate clothes, carrying her precious young child in one arm and a favorite book for leisure reading in the other.

It's during the fourth session with Janet that the counselor poses the question.

"Why can't you cry about what happened? What are you afraid will happen if you let yourself feel the full extent of the pain inside you?" Janet leans back in her chair and waits for Helen to speak.

Helen doesn't answer her right away; she feels as though an invisible wall inside her has risen up, silent as a ghost, when Janet asks her that. The wall separates Helen from the pain, from life "out there." To feel, to cry, would be to accept that Chrissy's death forever seals Helen into a kind of limbo from which she'd never be able to escape, never be able to resolve the overwhelming issue of whether her daughter went to her death hating her mother.

Helen couldn't live with that scenario.

She drives out to the small lake that's just beyond the border of the town on the east side. Now that Chrissy is in the second grade Helen has more time for herself, able to do things she's almost forgotten, things that she once knew how to do, like spending time alone, being quiet, talking to God.

Except these days it's a one-way conversation; she hasn't been able to hear from God lately. Not for a long time, really. Before her daughter was born she would spend time, hours, listening to God and talking to Him, pouring out her heart, thanking Him for giving her the kind of life she's always wanted.

But that was before, when Helen was under the illusion that God was somehow obligated to grant the wishes of her heart, to make life fit the pattern she's created in her mind ever since she was a young girl.

The lake is surrounded by trees, they're everywhere, providing a green haven at the lake's edge that Helen considers "her" place, a special spot where she can sit quietly, no one to interrupt or bother her (like Chrissy, she thinks), and reflect about her life.

Lately Helen has been feeling a kind of desperation about her life. It's not working out the way she thought it would. If she's honest with herself, Helen is afraid: afraid that she's out of control, that God has let go of her, detached from her. Why?

Because she's not grateful for the life she has been given, as difficult as it has been since the birth of her daughter. But she thinks that the friction, the clashes between Chrissy and her, aren't an excuse to not be grateful.

If only she knew the answer. Helen bows her head, lets herself get quiet, lets go of the wandering thoughts about what the rest of the day might hold for her, and focuses on listening to God.

"Lord, will You show me a sign, something that will let me know what Your will is for my life? I'm so afraid that I've somehow gotten off the path You want for me. So please speak to me in whatever way You want."

Helen waits; she waits what for her is a long time, listening to the *sotto voce* background sounds of birds gossiping in the trees. She envisions where the birds are perched by how their voices grow or fade in volume as they move from tree to tree, compact flashes of brown feathers, an occasional burst of red, flitting by her.

She chastises herself for losing focus and tries again to center, to get quiet before God. But there's no voice of God. There's nothing except the intermingling voices of the birds.

She has her answer for Janet when she returns to the counselor's office. Helen likes the way Janet doesn't try to make small talk or put on a fake friendliness for someone she hardly knows. The counselor sits quietly in her chair and waits for Helen to start. Janet has, she decides, grown to be like a good friend after all, someone she can share things with and not worry if she'll be discounted or told that she simply needs to trust God more in order for her problems to go away.

"Last week you asked me what I'd need to be able to let go of, to release what's inside me." Helen pauses and looks at Janet, who, as usual, is impassive, but in a nice way. She waits for Helen to continue, doesn't put any pressure on her to get on with it. Helen knows she can take as much time as it takes without fear of displeasing her.

Well," she finally says, "I need a sign from God that Chrissy didn't go to her death angry at me." She looks at Janet for a long time "That's it," she says. "A sign."

Rob wants them to accept the invitation the Wohlbergs gave to join them for dinner after the group meeting this Tuesday. They have gotten to know a few of the couples in the group, the ones who don't push themselves onto them, wanting to pool their shared grief and swim in the sea of pain that surrounds all of them.

The Wohlbergs are quiet, and Rob knows that Helen is attracted by their unobtrusive demeanor, the calm way Rick and Arlene talk about their son, a victim of black ice and too much speed on a dangerous curve last winter. He was a year older than Chrissy and that is a bond: they all understand the difficulty of raising a teenager in today's world.

"Oh, all right. I guess so," Helen says without enthusiasm when Rick pushes her to make a decision about the dinner invitation. Rick and Arlene know a restaurant, quiet, like them, where they can talk and get to know one another. Helen isn't sure she wants to get close to the Wohlbergs; she's not ready to open herself up to people who live on the outside of her wall, the one, by the way, that Janet saw (she told Helen in a later session) when she first met her at the group, almost two months ago.

Janet has suggested that they take a break, as she terms it, from the counseling for a while. She wants to give Helen time to listen for God's answer to the request Helen has made for a sign. Also, Christmas is approaching and life will get busy for them both.

But in actuality Helen knows it's up to her to either move ahead with her life or stay stuck in the pain and unresolved grief. But Helen prefers to think that it's really up to God. The ball is in His court.

The restaurant is pleasant and the seating is laid out so that everyone has their own private space around the tables and booths. Helen likes that and also the subdued lighting; it makes the illusion of anonymity easier to accept, and that's important for her.

The dinner is good and Helen is relieved to find that Rick and Arlene seem to respect her quietness and intermittent participation in the conversation. She also likes the way the Wohlbergs talk about their journey through the terrain of loss; they've been dealing with it for almost a year longer than she and Rob have.

They are lingering over their coffees after the dessert dishes are cleared, comfortable with not having to manufacture awkward conversation to fill silences. Arlene reaches down to her purse and pulls out a thick envelope; she asks if they'd like to see pictures of their son, Jeremy.

Rob says yes, but Helen barely nods; she's not really sure she wants to see them. It might threaten her wall by dragging up memories of dead children. Since she's sitting next to Arlene, she is the one to take each picture, glancing at it before passing it along to Rob. They are pictures of the Wohlberg's son in different settings: with his friends; with family members; at home in his room; Christmas last year with his parents. Rick and Arlene don't seem to be struggling with the fact that their son is no longer there, they talk as though he's still alive.

As Helen glances at the photo Arlene has just handed her, she stiffens and suddenly she can't breathe. Helen is unable to move for what seems like an eternity, but when she does it's to scream in a voice that she never imagined could be so loud. She jumps to her feet, photo still in hand, and clambers over Rob, clumsily stumbling toward the exit of the restaurant, barely able to keep her footing.

The universe has stopped, time is suspended, reality has come crashing down around her. Other patrons in the restaurant turn around in their seats to stare at this woman who's seemingly gone crazy, shrieking at the top of her voice as she dashes through the door, caroming off people trying to enter the restaurant.

Rob is not far behind, pursuing his wife, afraid to think of what is happening to her. He finds her around the back side of the restaurant, leaning against the wall, crying hysterically, the tears soaking the front of her blouse.

"What's wrong, Honey?" he asks, but she is crying so hard that she can't answer him. All she can do is wave the picture still gripped in her hand in his direction. She sobs, gasping for breath, unable to speak. When she opens her mouth it's to take in huge lungfuls of air, like a drowning person who has struggled up to the surface. Rick and Arlene stand outside at the corner of the building, keeping a respectful distance from Helen. A growing knot of people inside the restaurant cluster around the window and peer at the scene with undisguised curiosity. Rick and Arlene wave away the concerned manager; it's all right, they'll take care of it. They know from past experience that Helen is in the throes of intense grief.

But they're wrong: it's not grief (although the pain is being released, escaping like gas from a runaway balloon). It's joy, it's relief. When Helen finally gets her breath and the tears slow down enough for her to speak between convulsive sobs, she shows Rob the picture clutched in her hand.

The Wohlberg's son is standing in the foreground, the town's high school behind him. Off to the left side of the picture, not that far from Jeremy, a dark green Honda Accord is parked at the curb, several people standing around the car. One of them, an attractive girl in a brown suede jacket and jeans, is looking right at the camera, a broad smile on her face, a veritable picture of happiness. It's Chrissy.

Helen doesn't hear it out loud; the voice comes from within her, from the depths of her soul. She's heard it before, a familiar voice. "See," it says. "Here is your sign."

The Lion and the Hyena

The dust was heavier than usual that year.

Charles squinted up at the sun, a small white disk suspended nearly overhead, paler than the full moon. He thought to himself how much the sky looked like fog. The dust did that: muted everything—sky, sun, trees, horizon.

Kwami, leaning back in his chair, with his guileless West African smile that lit up his face from ear to ear said, "Oh, you *Yovos!*" (mixing French and Ewe). "You are too separated from nature to feel comfortable in our weather." Then his gentle laugh, almost a giggle.

This was harmattan season, when the winds from Europe, homesick for the southern ocean, swept over the Sahara and stole a fine layer of sand from its surface, then rained it down as a gentle white dust over African lands as far south as the Gulf of Guinea.

Charles had wiped the surface of the living room table two hours earlier; it was now tinted ash-gray with a fresh layer. The dust got into everything; he had to keep the windows closed against it, otherwise it drifted in as silent as the night and tainted his world with its soft, gritty presence. When he picked up a tumbler from the counter, it left the memory of its circular shape outlined in dustless contrast, like the faintly-remembered splatter paintings of leaves he had done in Kindergarten.

He had met Kwami during his second year in West Africa, at the Ewe Class offered through the German Consulate. The attaché at the American Embassy had suggested that it would enhance his standing with the locals if Charles knew some phrases in their own language. Kwami, an

Ewe from eastern Ghana, was the teacher; they'd developed a liking for one another almost from the start.

"*Yovo*," Kwami had explained to him, "is our Ewe word for foreigner. It means 'clever dog.' In our culture the dog represents a smart, quick person. So you White people are just like the clever dog, always doing something new and intelligent—like flying to the moon, or going under the water with your submarines."

Kwami exemplified the West African male: shorter than most Westerners, he was slight of build, with an impossibly narrow waist, a light milk-chocolate complexion, and an infectious smile and gentle laugh. His facial features were finely chiseled, the heritage of Western blood stealing into his ancestry.

"But this is too striking," Kwami told him at their first meeting. "Your name is 'Charles,' which was my French name. May I call you 'Charles?' " Kwami gave it the flowing French pronunciation that sounded like the effortless cascading of a waterfall.

"When the French were the colonial presence here," Kwami explained, "all Africans employed in government service, as I was, were given French *prénoms*, or first names. My boss renamed me 'Charles,' presumably for General de Gaulle." But when Kwami's country gained independence in the early sixties, he reclaimed his African name.

Charles had drifted to this part of West Africa after spending several aimless years as a Foreign Service Officer posted in out-of-the-way countries that changed their names with each edition of the Encyclopedia Britannica. When he was still in school the idea of working overseas seemed romantic. Now he tended to agree with Paul Theroux's observation that travel was fascinating only after you'd done it and were back home.

If he felt a lack of personal identity, Charles did have an affinity for learning languages. He soon became interested not only in Ewe, but also in the Africans' way of life. He had invited Kwami to his apartment just off the rue de l'Indépendence that Saturday afternoon to talk about African culture. Kwami was pleased to learn that his namesake wanted to learn more about the local people.

"Oh, my friend," he told him, "that is marvelous. That is very good." Leaning forward in his chair toward Charles, Kwami said: "Here is what I propose: let us go for a trip to my village. Yes, there you will see real African culture—how my people live, just as they always have for centuries."

Charles reluctantly agreed to Kwami's suggestion that they travel the African way to the village, by bush taxi. "Just take the mere necessities," Kwami had advised him. "Not as you *Yovos* usually do— transporting your Western culture on your back everywhere you go. This will be a genuine African experience." Then he smiled the broad, slow grin that made it hard for Charles to take offense.

They planned to meet at the bus park the following Friday afternoon and leave for Kwami's upcountry village for the weekend.

"Oh, my friend," Kwami said, rising from the chair. "This is an experience you will never forget! You are going to see an Africa that the *Yovo* never experiences. My family will be honored to meet you."

Charles walked the several blocks from the embassy to the bus park, a dusty stretch of ground adjacent to the Grand Marché, the large concrete building that served as the city's central market. People milled around in aimless confusion, some carrying battered pasteboard suitcases, others with large cloth sacks done up in a bundle on their heads. The noise and heat were disorienting; Charles regretted the loss of his apartment's air-conditioning for the weekend.

He looked for buses, but saw only oversize vans, most of them dented and scruffy, but colorful in their hand-painted bold, primary hues. He heard his name shouted above the din and turned around. Kwami was hurrying through the crowd, smiling and waving at him, carrying a pair of upside down chickens by their feet in his left hand.

"Kwami, you said we were traveling light," he said, pointing to the pair of inverted, disgruntled chickens.

"Oh, but these are a gift to my father. Lesson number one, my friend: the visitor always brings the host a gift. It is expected." Again the disarming smile.

During the trip north on the narrow two-lane blacktop Kwami supplied a running commentary on the flora, fauna, villages, and mythologies associated with the locales they passed. The scenery changed from flat coastal plains with open grassy fields, to gentle rolling hills as they traveled towards the northwest part of the country. A little farther on the hills mounted up, vivid red-brown slashes marking fields cut out of the dense vegetation on their slopes. Impossibly tall African trees that flourished under the combination of equatorial sun and abundant seasonal rains dominated the horizon.

Kwami pointed out an occasional red cloth flag on a tall pole in the middle of a field or clearing. "Places of magic," he said. "The flags are put there by the *vaudou* priests as a warning."

They got off the bus at an outdoor market in a town nestled in a crease of a hill. Heavy gray clouds, pregnant with rain, hovered just above the towering treetops. Kwami led them to a battered red Toyota pickup with a cracked fiberglass cover over the back. "This is our transport to the village," he said. The driver and Kwami had an animated discussion; Charles made out one or two Ewe words, but little else. They were to leave in half an hour.

Charles didn't see much of the trip to the village, other than a restricted view through the back of the pickup of the red dirt road trailing behind them and snatches of hillside terraces. His back began to ache from the combination of sitting on the rough wooden bench and the jolting of the vehicle over frequent potholes in the road.

When they stopped, the air had turned cool and fresh. Recent rains left soggy puddles scattered in the red earth. They walked up a path through tall grass and came to a grouping of a dozen mud-brown grass-thatched huts, arranged in a rough circle in the middle of a clearing. Dark towering trees formed a somber backdrop around the perimeter of the village. People were gathered in the clearing, some squatting around a smoldering fire that gave off a pungent smell of wood smoke. They were clothed in a variety of styles: men in faded dark trousers and long-sleeved shirts; women in traditional African wrap-around printed dresses. Several of the people looked up in recognition as Kwami approached their gathering, shouting out greetings that Charles gratefully recognized from his Ewe lessons.

A handful of small children came running up from one of the huts and circled around Charles, eyeing him with a mixture of curiosity and fear. They were naked, but didn't seem conscious of it. He smiled down at them, but they stared back with apprehension and suspicion.

"They think that White people are ghosts," Kwami said. "They're afraid of you." He let out a sudden burst of Ewe directed at the children, who responded by running away, trailing screams of terror as they went.

"What did you say to them?" Charles asked.

"I told them that you were a White Spirit who smiled at children before eating them."

Later he and Kwami relaxed around the fire after a dinner of *fou-fou*—ground cassava topped with a spicy peanut sauce. The men squatted on worn logs, but had insisted on bringing out a derelict wooden chair for Charles, who as Kwami's friend was the guest of honor. The women sat grouped together just outside the circle of light, talking in hushed voices. The dancing flicker from the fire lit up half-shapes of huts emerging from the pitch darkness. From the edge of the forest came a symphony of chirpings and clickings of night insects. He felt an unaccustomed quietness in his heart, a gentle peace that settled over him like the mantle of darkness from the mountain that enveloped the village.

Behind him a woman's voice broke the spell of stillness; she spoke loudly, but Charles couldn't understand the words. He looked up from the hypnotic glow of the fire and saw a dark shape coming toward him. He felt a sudden pang of fear as he remembered Kwami's talk about ghosts and *vaudou* priests. The dark shape moved with confidence and a steady rhythm, emerging from the canopy of night into the circle of flickering orange firelight. He was about to get to his feet and retreat, when he recognized the shadowy shape as a person.

She was clad in designer jeans and a bright colored floral print blouse, a knapsack was draped over one shoulder and a portable radio-cassette player dangled from her hand. A broad grin lit up her face as she spoke a word of greeting to the people, who by this time were on their feet and shouting out welcomes. She was about the same height as Kwami, and with the same slim build; her hair was braided in the fashionable way chosen by modern African women, but pulled back from her face. She strode directly into the knot of enthusiastic people gathered around the fire and began embracing them.

Kwami motioned for Charles to come over. "My friend," he said, "let me present to you my sister, Michelle." Kwami's face was bathed in a broad smile as he held his sister's arm.

"I'm very pleased to meet you," Charles said. He had never heard his friend speak of a sister. But Michelle did resemble Kwami, with her finely chiseled facial features, straight nose, high cheekbones, and creamy chocolate skin. Her dark eyes sparkled in the firelight.

Michelle lowered her pack and boom box to the ground, and held out her hand. "Likewise, I'm sure." She had a soft, throaty voice, and held his gaze without wavering. Her handshake was firm, but yielding. "And how is it that you are here in our village?" A slight frown wrinkled her forehead.

"Oh, he is one of my students," Kwami explained. "He wants to learn more about our African culture, so I proposed a weekend here. What do you think?"

She did not answer immediately, but looked coolly at Charles. "It is not often we find Westerners—she used the word 'Europeans'—who are truly interested in our people."

Her dark eyes transfixed Charles; he couldn't stop looking into them. They had a depth you could get lost in.

"And do you come here often?" he asked. He felt awkward, trying to fill the confusion he felt with conversation.

"Oh no," she said. "I'm usually buried under my studies, especially on the weekend. I go to the university. I'm studying to be a medical doctor."

"Yes," chimed in Kwami. "We are all very proud of my little sister. She is the one who will achieve great things for our family." Again Kwami laughed his little giggle.

Then Michelle was swept away by the villagers and her family, but Charles stayed on the outside of the group watching her lithe form retreat, illuminated by the light from the flickering fire.

They made a threesome the next day, touring the different neighborhoods of the village, and wandering into the dark green forest of giant trees. Kwami pointed out the path that led down to the river, the only source of water for the village. He and Michelle showed Charles places where they had played as children. He learned that her African name was 'Adamena,' but that she had chosen her French name from the popular Beatles' song of the 60s. Michelle wore a colorful African print dress of yellows and greens; her lustrous hair hung to her shoulders in lanky black braids that glistened in the sunlight.

The weekend passed too fast for Charles, lost in a timeless haze of being with Michelle. Her initial coolness toward him changed little by little to accepting smiles. Although Kwami accompanied them most of the time, Charles was only vaguely aware of his presence, so engrossed was he in Michelle. She was interested to find out that he was American ("But you speak French so *well*," she said), and asked what other countries he had served in. He told her of his disillusionment with the vocation he'd chosen, and hinted at his search for self-meaning.

When she spoke, Michelle looked right at him, unlike most Africans who are careful not to look into the other person's eyes. Kwami had explained to him that Africans considered this imposed directness an insult. She laughed a lot, and so did he. He began to love everything about the village, and about her.

And then it was time to return to the city.

When Kwami said that his sister would accompany them on the trip back, Charles could hardly suppress a surge of joy. But he just smiled and nodded his head. Brother and sister said goodbyes to their parents, and Charles to the friends he'd made. They trudged down the path to the main road, accompanied by a string of chattering children, now fearless in the *Yovo's* presence. Charles walked alongside Michelle and they talked easily and of nothing. He learned where she lived, and Michelle slipped him her telephone number while Kwami was talking with the driver of the bush taxi.

Charles sat beside her all the way from the village to the capitol. By the time they arrived at the bus park, he knew he was in love. Michelle flagged a taxi to her apartment, smiled and waved goodbye. Charles looked with longing at the vehicle until it disappeared in the haze of heat and exhaust fumes, then turned to walk to his own place.

"My friend, can I accompany you to your apartment?" Kwami asked.

"Sure," Charles said. "Time to re-enter civilization with a 'Coca,' right?" He already knew of Kwami's fondness for Coca-Cola. Once in the apartment, Kwami stood with discomfort, shifting his weight from one foot to the other.

"I need to tell you something about our African culture," he said. "May I talk with you?"

"Certainly. What do you have for me to learn?"

"We have an old saying—a proverb, you'd call it. 'The hyena does not run with the lion.'" Kwami glanced up at Charles' face, then back to the floor. "Do you understand what this means?"

"Well . . . no. I'm not sure."

"It means," Kwami said, "that different peoples cannot mingle together. The hyena lives separate from the lion because they are different breeds." Kwami's voice took on a seriousness that Charles had not heard before.

"I see you are attracted to my sister. And she is also attracted to you." Kwami looked straight at him. "But such a thing can never be. Our family would not permit it. Michelle will marry one of her own—someone from our tribe. It will be for our parents to decide whom."

He turned to leave, then paused at the door. "You are new to our culture. You didn't know. Now I have told you, and now you know what must be done."

Charles stood in the doorway, feeling waves of emotion like the swell of the ocean sweep over him as he watched his friend leave. He hadn't said a word in reply, but now powerful feelings surged in him: indignation, then anger. Who was Kwami to tell him what to do? And his family—living in a bygone era of social conduct that was completely out of touch with the present—who were they to dictate to him? Michelle was a thoroughly modern woman, and she'd do what she wanted.

It was partly out of this reaction, but mostly out of rebellion, that Charles telephoned Michelle the next day. He suggested they meet at a restaurant near the university for dinner. She looked stunning in a dark cotton dress with a pattern of tiny white print flowers. Charles felt himself floating off the floor and entering a euphoric world of gauzy soft lights, with Michelle's warm brown face at its center.

They had their first kiss two days after their return from Michelle's village, and then saw each other daily for several weeks. Charles felt carried along by something completely out of his control; he couldn't alter or interrupt the magic—not that he wanted to. But they both had concerns.

"Charles," Michelle said one evening when they were together at his apartment. "I have heard from my parents, through my brother." Her usually serene face was furrowed in concern. "They disapprove of our relationship." She was silent after this.

Charles was silent also, staring at, but not seeing, the woven beige mat on the floor. He held her hands in his, feeling the exciting warmth of her body next to him.

"I'll talk to your brother. I'll talk to your parents if need be. I'll make them understand. Michelle . . ." He hesitated. "For the first time in my life, I feel complete and fulfilled—all because of you."

"No, *cheri*, it's you who doesn't understand," she said in a voice edged with sharpness. "You don't know what it is like for me. In our culture children must obey their parents—no matter what." She began sobbing quietly. "Why can't they just let me live my life the way I want?"

Charles had no answer for her, other than to hold her in his arms. They sat there as darkness crept in, filling the apartment with unfeeling shadows.

He had to be away from the capitol on business for the next few days, but promised to call her when he returned. The minute he got back, in fact. That was why he was surprised when there was no answer when he phoned her apartment. He redialed to make sure, but again, no answer. Maybe the phone's out, he thought, it happens here all the time. You never know when the power, or the water, or the phones will go on the blink.

He drove to her apartment near the university. There was no answer when he knocked. He put his ear to her door, but it was quiet inside. No, the neighbors hadn't seen her for several days. No, M'sieur, she didn't say if she was leaving on a trip.

He decided on the spur of the moment to drive to Kwami's place, an unassuming little house behind a high gray wall with an iron gate. Kwami let him in.

"Where is your sister?" Charles said. "Have you heard from her in the past several days?"

Kwami avoided Charles' gaze and looked at the floor before he spoke.

"She has returned to the village. Michelle will not be seeing you again. It is forbidden by my parents." Kwami then stared at Charles and spoke in slow, somber tones. "Please, my friend. Do not try to find her. Forget her and go on with your life. Your relationship cannot be. You do not understand our African way of life."

Charles didn't remember much after that. Over Kwami's protests he pushed past him and sprinted to his car. He drove until he found the road going north, the one that led to Michelle's village. He didn't think about what he would do once he got there, only that he *had* to get there, and as soon as he could.

The journey passed in a blur of towns, people, and domestic animals grazing in open pastures. The fields yielded to hills, and the hills became mountains; all of this passed before his eyes, barely registering in his mind. He got lost in one town, and spent precious minutes searching for the road leading to the village. Finally, he stopped and asked some men by the side of the road—he was fortunate to remember the name of her village from his first visit—and got directions. As he drove he tried to remember landmarks that he'd glimpsed from the back of the pickup truck.

Then the rain started, a fine, steady mist that swirled out of the gray clouds skimming the treetops. Charles almost missed the dirt road leading to the village; the grass at the entrance had grown higher. He parked his car on the shoulder and ran toward the village. Halfway up the path, he stopped to catch his breath. What was he going to do once he came to the clearing, what was he going to say? He'd think of something.

Just as he emerged into the clearing, two things happened at almost at the same time. He felt a sudden heaviness in his limbs, as though his legs and arms weighed a thousand pounds. His brisk pace became a staggering struggle to remain upright and not topple into the wet grass. He saw a man in front of him across the clearing: his wild, ragged hair stuck out in unkempt shards. He held a long wooden shaft in his right hand, and was naked except for a worn leather tunic around his waist, and a belt adorned with colored feathers. His face was painted in white and red stripes, with circular swirls of color around the eyes. The man was chanting something in a language Charles didn't recognize, and as he chanted, Charles felt heavier and heavier.

He tried to call out, but no sound came. It was like a recurring nightmare from childhood in which he was running in fear through a world bathed in heavy syrup, trying to call out, but his mouth seemed paralyzed. Charles saw several people from the village standing behind the man, whom he now recognized as a *vaudou* priest. One of them was Michelle's father. Charles sank to his knees, as though pressed down under an immense weight.

He made one last supreme effort to speak, and cried out with surprising strength.

"Michelle!"

He tried again, his words cutting through the misty air.

"Michelle! I love you!"

His vision started to blur, and dark, dancing spots rose before his eyes. As though in a dream, enacted in slow motion from under a leaden gray sea that now muffled his hearing, he saw a woman appear behind the group of men, then advance toward Michelle's father. She spoke quick, unintelligible words, then reached up to the printed cloth head covering she was wearing and pulled it free, throwing it to the ground. It was Michelle.

She said something else, and ran to where Charles knelt in the damp grass.

"*Cheri*, I am here," she said. He felt the closeness of her presence, smelt her fragrant sweetness as she embraced him.

In an instant Charles felt the crushing weight lift. The world came into focus and the under-the-sea pressure in his ears cleared. He heard the chanting of the priest, the yapping of dogs in the village, and Michelle's sobs as she drew him close.

"I love you, Charles," she said. "But you must know that my place is here—with my parents, my people. You were wrong to have come." She paused and looked into his eyes. "I will always remember how you touched my heart. But you belong to your world; that is your identity. Mine can be nowhere but here." She indicated the forest, the hills, the people around her.

They rose from the grass, looked into each other's eyes, then parted hands. While Michele turned back to face the villagers, Charles walked in a slow, but steady pace down the path towards his car, away from her. The rain began to fall in large, heavy drops around him, an insistent drumbeat, bathing his hair with its wetness and forming streams of water that ran down his face. They mixed with his tears, then fell to the ground and joined the harmattan dust in making small rivulets running down the hillside.

Pastorale

A fantasy on *The Meadow* by Claude Monet (1840-1926)

The road is hardly distinguishable now. Years of disuse have left it partially hidden under an obscuring camouflage of tall grasses and wildflowers that have grown unchecked over time. Only if you knew it was there, and looked closely through the tangled web of dense, shaded growth, could you make out the faint tracks that seem to suggest an ancient rutted pathway in the ochre-toned earth. The brown soil harbors a suggestion of wheel ruts that time and the weather have almost erased; they trace a path, now nature-hidden, through the fields and then disappear into the distance.

On the left a tall stand of wind-blown cypress rise up, vertical spires of dusty green whose serrated tops sway back and forth in the hot summer breezes. Further off on the left is another stand; these slender trees reach upward to form a verdant backdrop that contrasts with the brilliant blue summer sky. Stately white cumulus clouds billow and expand like living beings, cavorting in the afternoon heat. On the right a lush green meadow spreads outward from our view, creating a natural line of demarcation between the grasses and wildflowers. Fences aren't needed here: nature and man's plans work together to provide their own harmonious boundaries.

At the far reach of the meadow clusters of dun-colored cows stand grouped together, heads down as they graze the luxuriant grass. Beyond them conical stacks of hay squat on the landscape like straw-colored tropical huts, basking in the meridonial sun. Further in the distance more trees stake their claim to the soil. They are widely interspersed in the outlying fields, the green-yellow masses with large spread-out branches bear wide leaves that provide a canopy of welcome shade for the habitat underneath, both flora and fauna.

Where the sky comes down to the horizon a hazy blue range of hills rises up in the distance, a solid presence, like an anchor that holds the scene intact. They stretch to the very edges of the far-off fields, marking the end of the valley. Beyond them is another world—a place with towns and cities, people and automobiles, jobs, pollution, hurry, and not enough time.

A lone figure stands in the midst of the tall grass and wildflowers; she wears a dark dress and a white blouse and on her head a tapered straw hat, matching the color of the sun-bleached grass that surrounds her. She is bent over, gently inclined to the earth, gathering flowers—brilliant reds and purples, along with the occasional whites—for this afternoon's dinner table. The sun rides just past the vertical; the shadows of the cypress begin to project dark lumpy forms that stretch across the ground.

The air is full of the slow, joyful noise of the countryside: cicadas, crickets, and grasshoppers chirping and whirring, together generating a musical accompaniment for the lively business of life growing under the warm, nurturing sun.

The woman turns and begins to walk off to her left towards the green meadow, deserting the tall grass and wildflowers. In the distance, coming steadily toward her, is the figure of a man. His appearance is foreshortened by the grand expanse of the far field; he is dwarfed by the stacks of hay and the occasional tree. It is Fernand, coming from his chores in the fields. He appears to grow gradually in height as he nears; finally the two figures meet in the middle of the pasture, where the stores of hay and cattle share common ground.

"*Bon jour*, good afternoon, Ma'm'selle Georgette," he says, deference hiding his emotions. He takes off his blue cloth farmer's cap and bows slightly towards the woman. His bared head reveals a shock of light-brown hair, tousled and askew in the gentle breeze that breathes across the meadow. He wears a sweat-stained red cloth around his neck, just above his coarse blue jersey.

"Yes, good afternoon, M'sieur Fernand," Georgette mummers, the straw hat nodding in his direction. She smiles slightly, her red lips turning up ever so gently at the corners. But Fernand does not see this gesture, hidden under the shadow of her hat.

They walk in silence for several minutes. "Here," she says abruptly, offering a lone yellow flower to Fernand. Now her head is raised, and Georgette looks at him directly. Her face is long and angular, her nose straight, but not broad like her father's, the owner of these fields. Her skin, shielded from the sun, is fair.

Fernand slows his pace slightly, taken aback by her sudden gesture. He recovers himself, returns her gaze, but dares not meet her eyes openly, and accepts the floral gift. "Thank you," he says, with a hint of a stammer. He speaks with the broad dialect of the country: lengthened vowels, each phrase ending in an uplifted tone, as if in a question. The folk in the towns beyond the hills make fun of their accent, but the farmer folk of the valley are proud of their language, their heritage. It's a trait that has been handed down for generations, a mark of distinction.

"Do you know what this flower is called?" she says in her soft voice, shy, but with a trace of humor—almost mocking—in her voice. She glances at Fernand for a moment, then answers the question for him. "Some call it the 'Valley Daisy,' but"—and she pauses imperceptibly, daring to regard him more fully in the face—"it's known, as you must be aware, as the 'Lover's Bouquet.' Did you know that?"

Fernand's face reddens, and he turns his gaze away from her, pretending to regard a tree at the edge of the pasture. He makes an impatient gesture with his hand, as if to wave away an offending fly.

"Of course," he replies brusquely, "that's something we both know from childhood. It was a childish pastime." Now Fernand turns and looks at her with a penetrating gaze; he makes no attempt to hide his emotions. "Don't you remember how we used to play that game? 'She loves me; she loves me not.'" Emboldened by his irritation, Fernand begins counting off the petals, roughly plucking each one from the center in turn: " 'She loves me, she loves me not; she loves me'. . . ."

Georgette reaches over and with a quick, but gentle, motion of her hand takes the flower from his hand. " 'She loves me not,' " she continues. Georgette glances up at Fernand, the same coy smile on her lips. "'She loves me,'" she says, removing the last yellow petal from the stem. She stops, looking up at him, her regard posing a question—or is it defiance?—one that is written on her face, as if challenging him.

"Yes!" he blurts out, in a voice filled with passion. "But your father. He would never permit . . ." here his voice trails off, losing its ardor. Fernand looks back at the ground, his statement unfinished, but understood.

"But have you asked him?" she says. Georgette reaches out and takes, not the torn flower, but Fernand's large farmer's hand in hers. "You might be pleasantly surprised," she adds. "You will see; we will go see him together."

The two figures continue across the meadow, walking towards the farmhouse in the distance, but now they are together, hand in hand. As they recede from view they seem to blend, to become one. Then they fade into the warmth of the meadow.

The Wound Licker

Josh came to us in a strange way.

One year in the late fall when the weather was debating about turning from a prolonged Indian Summer toward winter, I asked our son, Frederick, to go out to the barn and check on the hay we had laid up in the loft. I knew that we'd need to think about getting it down for winter feed and I wanted to be prepared when the cold weather finally came. He came back to the house after a short while with a question.

"Hey Dad, what kind of food do we have for dogs?"

"Dogs? We don't have any dogs, son."

"Well, we do now," Fred replied.

We live in what you'd call "the sticks." South Fork sits in the middle of a broad Midwestern plain that runs from Hunnicutt Valley all the way to the proud mountains in the north. There aren't a great many towns out here: small settlements are the general rule, a collection of maybe a dozen families clustered around a windmill and water tower, a store if you're lucky.

We do farming out here, and it's good land for that. There's no industry or factories of any kind within two hundred miles, so it's kind of desolate. Pioneers from the last century pushed through our area looking for minerals, hoping for gold. They didn't find anything that they thought worthwhile, so most of them kept on moving west. But some of those hardy folks decided to make a go of it here, using whatever skills they had brought with them from the countries they had left behind. Most of these emigrants knew how to farm the land.

Whole Cloth

I'm second generation from the Old Country. My folks had got caught up in the fever for gold and the new life it promised—like a lot of people around that time—so they made the long journey across the Atlantic hoping to become rich. But when they saw the springtime beauty of this land parading before them like a fine painting hanging on the wall of an art museum, they quickly gave up thoughts of traveling farther out West.

You have to remember the rugged conditions that pioneers faced back then. To complicate matters my folks were parents of a new baby—me. That helped change their minds about trekking around an uncivilized country, looking for gold that might have disappeared by the time they arrived in that far away land on the other side of the big mountains. Both of them had grown up in farming families back across the ocean so they knew what needed to be done.

Eventually some of the farmers decided to raise sheep and cattle to supplement the crops from the fields; pretty soon a lot of those living on the plains had livestock, as well as acreage given over to crops. Obviously, fences needed to be put up and it wasn't long before our little community could be measured by how many miles of barbed wire had been strung and how many fence posts folks had planted in the stubborn soil, and not by the number of families living there. This was the environment I was raised in and the kind of farm I ended up inheriting when my folks passed on.

And it was on this farm that Fred told me that day about his discovery of the mysterious appearance of the dogs.

"One just gave birth out in the barn while I was there," he said. "Don't know how they got in, but there's two of them, besides the puppy."

This was before we had electricity run out to the barn, so there were places where the shadows were deep, especially in the corners. Fred had heard sounds from one of those dark corners—at first it spooked him—so he decided to investigate. Fred, being first-born, is strong-willed and independent, so he didn't think too much about being by himself in a dark barn. He wasn't afraid of what he might find there.

When he walked over to where the sound was coming from and his eyes got adjusted to the shadows, he saw two dogs curled up against the thick wooden wall. Well, one was curled up; the other was lying on its side, panting heavily.

Kids who grow up on a farm are a lot different than city kids. I'm not saying they're better, it's just that being on the farm they see a lot more of what you'd call "life." In other words Fred was used to seeing animals being born and he pretty well understood the whole process. It didn't take him but a minute to realize that the one dog was in heavy labor and was about to give birth right there in the corner.

He grabbed an old blanket that we had hanging on the wall, a tattered spread that we kept for use in winter, and carefully laid it next to the momma dog that was in the throes of labor. The other dog—had to have been have been the papa, he figured—got to its feet and looked at Fred, not in an unfriendly way, but like it was making sure he didn't do anything hurtful to his mate. Fred slid the blanket under the momma as best he could, all the time murmuring words of reassurance and encouragement to both of them.

So that day Fred helped the momma dog give birth, and pretty soon the first puppy emerged. Fred picked it up and laid it next to the mother so that she could lick it and do whatever she needed to do for it, while Fred went back and stationed himself on the receiving end of the dog, waiting for the next one to come out. But there was only one puppy born that day. Fred checked pretty carefully to ensure that there weren't others waiting to be born, because most dogs have a litter of about four or five puppies—depending on the breed.

But that was it, only one puppy. He made sure momma and the newborn were comfortable, then he came back to the house. After he told me about our visitors, we found an old bag of cat food we kept around for feeding the occasional farm mouser; we figured that cats and dogs couldn't be that much different in the kind of food they ate. Anyway beggars can't be choosers.

We trudged out to the barn, and I let Fred go in first; I didn't want to spook the dogs by showing up unannounced, and a stranger to boot.

"What kind of dogs are they, Dad?"

I looked at them: both were longhaired, with fairly long snouts, especially the dog that I took to be the father. I'm no expert, but I hazarded a guess.

"I dunno, son. Sorta looks like the one, the male, is a kind of Collie. But I'm not sure about that. There are so many breeds of dogs; these two look like they're mixed."

For some reason we were talking in low, hushed voices, the kind you'd use in church. Maybe we just didn't want to upset the new arrival, and especially the momma who had just given birth.

"You know what's strange?" Fred said.

"Well son, lots of things in this world are strange. Which one are you talking about?"

Fred smiled at my feeble attempt to make a joke. "I've never heard of a dog's mate accompanying the female, especially when she's about to give birth. Have you?"

I thought about that for a minute, but finally had to admit that, no, I'd never run across that particular circumstance before, nor had I ever heard of it. We stood there for a few minutes and looked at the trio: mother, father, and baby. Momma looked like she was taking good care of her newborn; her mate seemed proud and protective.

Over the next several days Fred and I made regular visits out to the barn to check on the dogs; they seemed to be getting along okay. I think papa and momma were grateful for our care. The big question for me was where the dogs had come from. We checked with our neighbors, but none had any dogs missing. Those two just seemed to have come out of nowhere.

"So what do you want to name him, son?" I asked Fred. "You're the one that found them, and you helped bring him into the world. Seems right that you should name that pup."

" 'Josh,' " he said without any hesitation.

When I asked him why that name, he sort of shrugged his shoulders. "It just seems to me it's a name that fits him. He's a 'Josh.'"

So from then on his name was Josh, and pretty soon the pup began responding when we called his name. Of the two of us, Fred spent the most time around the dog and they bonded quickly. I tried to coax the male dog out of the barn so he would help round up some of the stray sheep that were always wandering off; he would come to the door of the barn and look out, but I couldn't get him to venture out any further. It's like he didn't want to leave his mate and little offspring.

Some time after that Fred and I were out working in the east field, repairing the fence posts and barbed wire before the really cold weather set in. There's always hard, tedious work to be done on a farm, and ours was no exception. By this time Josh was old enough to get around by himself and would often leave the shelter of the barn and his parents to accompany us on our chores.

This day he had come as far as the field where we were working, but Josh was interested in playing and exploring gopher holes. He would stick his little snout down the hole, sniff around, and then pull it out with his nose covered with dirt and brambles from his investigations. But this didn't discourage him, and he made great sport out of rushing at the holes as though he were going to trap some critter there and drag him out.

We were stretching a length of barbed wire between posts, replacing a section that had finally rusted out under the effects of successive seasons of sun, rain, and snow. Fred went back to the truck to get another box of fence staples and I was using the tool we call a "come-along" to stretch the wire to the right tension. I guess that I took my eyes off the wire for a moment, reaching down to pick up a handful of staples from the old box, when the come-along slipped. The barbed wire whipped back and raked across the upper part of my left leg, laying open a six-inch length of skin in a diagonal line.

I let out a yelp and automatically grabbed my leg, but the blood was already starting to flow through the rip in the jeans and run to the ground. At first I only felt a burning sensation, but then the hurt began to set in and the wound started to throb. Fred rushed over from the truck, a look of concern in his eyes.

"Dad, what is it?" But he could see what had happened as well as I could from the snaked length of barbed wire resting on the ground and the come-along still dangling midway down the offending portion of the wire.

"Dang, I wasn't watching what I was doing, Son. Goes to show . . ." but I let the sentence trail off. Both of us knew the costly mistake my inattention had brought me. "Guess we'd better get back to the house and call Doctor Phelps." I glanced down at the bleeding leg wound and then at Fred's face. He knew this was going to take more than a Band-Aid to fix.

I hitched myself up in the truck on the passenger side, grabbing an old shirt crumpled in a corner to put under my leg so the blood wouldn't seep into the seat cover, while Fred climbed in the driver's side. He paused for a moment and whistled for Josh to get in with us, since we were a good distance, in puppy terms, from the house. Once Josh clambered into the cab, Fred let out the clutch and we roared away, bouncing over the gopher mounds and rocking sideways over the uneven ground.

Josh hopped up onto the seat between Fred and me and gave a curious look at my leg, then at my face. I was gripping the door handle tightly, partly to keep from bouncing around too much in the jolting truck, but also to have something to hold onto against the ever-mounting pain from the wound. I was concentrating on dealing with the pain, my eyes partly closed, so I didn't feel Josh's small tongue licking at my leg at first. When I opened my eyes he was beside me, bent over my leg and gently lapping at the wound.

Whole Cloth

I pushed him away, afraid that his mouth carried things that would infect the gash, but because Fred was driving so fast across the field, I had to spend more time just trying to hold on than fend the dog away from my leg. Fred pulled up to the house in a proverbial cloud of dust, and my wife, seeing the truck careening across the field, had come out on the front porch, a look of concern written on her face.

Fred jumped out of the truck as soon as he braked to a stop and came around to the passenger door. "Let me help you out, Dad," he said, his own face mirroring my wife's apprehension. I gingerly slid my legs out of the truck cab and lowered myself to the ground. I expected it to hurt like the dickens when I put weight on my injured leg, but I was surprised to find that the effects of the wound didn't pain me like I thought they would. I walked stiff-legged to the house, Fred supporting me on one side and Margene on the other, so that I wouldn't break open whatever fragile clotting had taken place in the scant few minutes it had taken us to drive from the fence line to our house.

Fred told his mom to call the doctor once they had me inside the house and settled in a kitchen chair. While she did that, Fred put another chair in front of me and carefully raised the bad leg onto it, so that it would be elevated. Again, I expected pain when we maneuvered my leg around, but there wasn't any, maybe just a twinge or two; nothing to complain about. Meanwhile, Josh had followed us into the house, a real no-no, for Margene had decreed long ago that her house would be animal free. Josh must have figured that she would be too busy to notice him, and he was right.

He stood at the base of my chair, looking up into my face; he had the most interesting look on his features, a mixture of curiosity and contentment. Yes, that's right:

contentment, if you can say that a dog can convey that emotion. Well, Josh sure did and I didn't mind so much that he'd violated Margene's rules by coming in with us. But she did, and after she discovered him there with us in the kitchen she unceremoniously shooed him outside.

Doc Phelps pulled up in his car about fifteen minutes later and came into the kitchen, black medical bag in hand. He was already eyeing my leg and I wasn't looking forward to the pain that was coming my way once he started examining the wound.

"Well, Cornell, let's take a look at what you did. Tell me now what happened," he said. While he talked he pulled on a pair of latex gloves and then took out a sharp-bladed knife from his bag to cut away my pants leg so as to expose the wound. It would have to be my good pair of jeans, the ones Margene had bought me last Easter, instead of the old ratty pair I kept crumpled up in my closet. Oh well.

So I told Doc how the come-along had slipped out of my hands or whatever, and the recoil of the tensioned barbed wire had sliced into me like a saw blade. I didn't want to look down at the wound, fearing what I'd see. Did I mention that I get sick at the sight of blood? Anyway, I sneaked a quick look at my leg while the doc was bent over it. There was a lot of dried blood around the wound that had formed a sort of thin scab over it, but the gash itself had stopped bleeding.

"Margene, do you have a clean cloth and some alcohol? I want to clean up this area and get a better look at the wound," Doc said. He was still bent over my leg, looking closely at something there. After he had swabbed off my upper leg, he handed the red-stained towel back to Margene, all the while peering at the place on my leg where the wound was. Then he straightened up at looked me right in the eyes.

"Cornell, what happened here?"

"Whaddya mean, Doc?" I answered.

"This is the darnedest thing I've ever seen," he said. "There's no wound; just a scar here. It's closed up."

I didn't say anything; what could I, after all? Doc was still looking right at me, but really it was like he was looking through me at something unseen that was the object of his thoughts. I finally looked at my leg. He had cleaned up the dried blood so that the pink of the flesh was showing through. There was a thin whitish sort of line running diagonally across the top of my leg; that's where the barbed wire had laid open the leg. Now it was only a scar.

"Doc, how could this be?" I said. "I was bleeding like a stuck pig. Fred saw it, didn't you, Son?"

Fred nodded. "Doctor, my dad's leg was cut open real bad; I saw it with my own eyes. He was bleeding pretty bad too."

Doctor Phelps just stood there, not saying anything for the longest while, still looking at my leg like he was judging the value of an expensive watch he was thinking of buying. Finally he just shook his head and looked at me.

"Well, I don't know what to make of this. It goes beyond what I learned in medical school and all my years of practice here. I was fixing to get you to the county hospital when I pulled up to your place. But now . . ."

"Dad, why don't you try to stand up and see how it feels," Fred said. "Can he do that, Doctor?"

So the two of them helped hoist me upright, holding me under the arms. I put most of my weight on the right leg and just tested out my left leg by letting it take a little weight, gradual like.

I looked up at Doctor Phelps. "It feels fine. It doesn't hurt at all. Well, maybe just a little twinge, but nothing like I expected it to." I tried taking a few tentative steps in the kitchen, putting more weight on it. Then I started parading around the room and ended up by stomping on the floor with my left leg. Doc came over and examined the leg again, but only shook his head in wonderment.

"It's a miracle, that's what it is!" Margene stood by the stove, looking at all of us, her eyes wide and a sort of defiant expression on her face. "Go on, you can't explain it any other way. God healed you, Cornell. I saw what that leg looked like when you first came in here."

"Well . . ." Doc seemed kind of reluctant to jump on that bandwagon, but I guess that was only natural for him, being a medical man trained in science, not theology. But he did go to the local Methodist church in town, just like we did. Anyway, he left our house still shaking his head, like he was in a kind of daze.

"Dad, I'll go back to the field and get our tools," Fred said.

I started to agree with him, but then a thought came to me and I stopped myself from what I was going to say.

"No son, we'll both go back to the field and finish up what we started. There's still enough light and we can get that section of the fence fixed up before it's time for dinner."

I looked at Margene, expecting her to put the quash on my idea, but she didn't. She nodded in agreement and said that if God had healed my leg, then I should be using it, not acting like it was still injured.

So that's what we did. I changed out of the cut-up jeans and put on the old pair. Josh was waiting for us on the porch and scampered along as we got back in the truck. I saw the old shirt still lying on the seat, dark red with blood. I wadded it up and tossed it in the truck bed, but couldn't get out of my mind what had just happened. That shirt was a powerful reminder of what had gone on that afternoon. Until I could see another explanation, I decided that I was going along with Margene and accept it as a miracle.

Little Josh sat between me and Fred, just like he had coming back to the house about an hour ago. But this time he kept looking up in my face with that almost human expression of intelligence in his eyes. I patted his head and told him that he was a good doggie. You see, that was before I knew what had happened, before we came to understand about Josh.

Then winter came in earnest, and then the snow was too deep for the truck to get through to the fields. The temperature hovered on the far side of zero so we didn't go out to the pastures that much. But on the days when the sun warmed things up enough to get out, Josh came with us in the truck or on foot, and even his dad started joining us on the journeys to the frozen pastures. Otherwise they stayed in the barn, which was warm enough, thanks to the cows that we wintered there. And as the season advanced, the snow began softening enough that we could make regular trips to the fields.

As time went on that wasn't the only thing softening. I noticed that Margene's heart started turning toward little Josh; she began letting him in the house from time to time. You could tell that she liked him, but there was something else going on, something we only learned about later.

"Well," she said, "I don't mind Josh being in here, as long as he stays in the kitchen with me. He's not like the other dogs we used to have, jumping on everything and everybody, drooling all over the place."

I would catch her from time to time talking to the dog when she thought no one else was around. Josh would sit on his haunches and gaze up at my wife, an interested look on his face, just like he was following the conversation— even though it was one-sided. Margene was talking to him like he was a human being and could understand everything she was saying. Maybe he could.

The next thing that happened came toward the end of that winter. By then we were getting occasional signs of the approaching spring, little tufts of green slowly pushing their way up through the remaining patches of snow in the pastures, as well as by the gradual lengthening of the days.

We had been working around the house, making some repairs to the siding after the winter had wreaked its corrosive effects on any wood that was exposed. Josh was there as usual, sitting on the porch by the stairs, supervising our work. Fred was helping me position a long piece of cedar under the eaves when we heard the muffled ringing of the telephone through the walls of the house. Pretty soon Margene came hurrying out to the porch, a worried look on her face.

"Cornell, that call was from the Watsons. Their little girl just fell out of a tree where she was playing with a friend. Frieda says her leg's broke real bad, the bone showing through. They tried calling Doc Phelps, but he's out on another call, so they need to get her to the hospital. Can we get the truck over there and drive her into town?"

The Watsons lived about five miles down the road from us. They hadn't done as well as we had the last couple of years, consequently they couldn't afford to keep their automobile running or get it fixed when it broke down. Naturally, Fred and I stopped working on the house and headed for the truck, Josh on our heels. I debated whether to take the dog along or not, but in the end we all piled in the pickup and started out for the Watson's place.

Most of the winter snow was gone from the roads, but in its place were sloughs of mud that made driving slow and slippery. We finally reached the Watson's farm and pulled in alongside the house. Frieda and Hugo, her husband, were standing on the porch; worry and concern had drawn their faces into taut lines.

"Thank you for coming," Frieda said, wiping her hands on the plain apron she wore over her dress. We had no other way of doing this . . ." Her voice trailed off into a corner of embarrassment, proud folks who hated to ask for help.

"Don't you worry about that, Frieda," I said. "We're only glad to help. Where's your little girl?"

"We got her inside, waiting for you to come," Hugo said, his eyes careful to not meet mine. "I put a sort of splint on her leg so as we can carry her out to your truck."

Fred and I followed them inside the house, but Frieda balked when she saw Josh trotting in with us. I don't know why I said it; maybe I was beginning to get an idea about Josh at this time, but for whatever reason I told her that he was well behaved and wouldn't get into anything in their house. Frieda's face wrinkled in disapproval, but because of the favor we were doing them, she grudgingly allowed Josh to come in with us.

Their child, a girl of about nine-years-old by the name of Anita, was lying on an old sofa that had a washed out floral pattern. Her leg was encased in two lengths of rough-hewn planks tied together by several loops of frayed clothesline. You could see that she was in pain, her tear-stained face distorted with the misery she was feeling. The lower part of her dress was stained dark red by the blood from where her leg bone was protruding from the wound. It looked like a white stick coming out of her right leg below the knee, at a place where nothing but pink skin should be.

I glanced over at Fred and he looked back at me, both of us silently wondering how we were going to get this little girl out to the truck and then somehow prop her in the cabin without hurting her more than she already had been hurt. I wasn't looking forward to making that first part of our journey from the house to the truck because that was going to be the most painful one for Anita. I felt squeamish in my stomach already after seeing that jagged piece of white bone sticking through her leg.

Fred and I got together with Hugo off a ways from the sofa; we didn't want his daughter to overhear us discussing our concerns about the best way to get her to the truck. We were mulling over several ideas about how to carry her, when I heard Frieda raise her voice in anger.

"You get away from her! Stop that right now!"

She ran toward the couch, an old newspaper rolled up in her hand to swat Josh with. He was by the couch, standing up on his hind feet with his front paws resting on the cushions. He was licking the place where the little girl's wound was, and the girl was looking at him with wonderment in her eyes, like she was watching a magic show.

I rushed over to intercept Frieda before she could hit Josh and grabbed her arm. I guess I was none too gentle at the time, but I sure didn't want her to scare Josh and certainly not to beat him. Something was telling me to not let her interfere with what Josh was doing.

"It's all right, Frieda. He doesn't mean any harm. He won't do anything to hurt her. Trust me on this."

147

Frieda didn't take too kindly to what I was telling her; she was going protect her daughter, just like any momma bear would protect her cubs or a dog her pups. I held on to her upraised arm till I felt it relax, but by that time Josh had finished whatever he was doing and lowered himself off the sofa. He went over to the corner by the kitchen and sat down, looking at me with that intelligent look in his eyes like he was trying to tell me something.

Hugo said that we'd better get Anita out to the truck, as time was wasting and we didn't want to be on the roads as the sun was going down. He turned back to his daughter and looked once more at her wound, at the place where the bone was sticking out. All of a sudden he stiffened and stopped dead in his tracks. I went over to see what was the matter. He was looking down at the wound where the blood had matted and had begun to turn a dark red.

What I saw made me feel a sudden tightening in my stomach, followed by a strange kind of tingling running down my back. Where the leg bone had been sticking out, there was nothing now except a covering of dried blood. Hugo glanced at his daughter.

"Honey, are you all right?" His voice had that stiff and strained sound that someone makes who is struggling to speak normally, but fighting against an overwhelming emotion rising up inside them.

"Yes, Daddy," she said. "I feel all right, I guess." She paused a bit, chewing on her lower lip, before going on. "My leg doesn't hurt as much as before." She gave her dad a tentative smile.

Hugo was staring at his daughter open-mouthed, unable to take in that which his eyes and mind were registering. I knew just what he felt like, having experienced something similar several months before. It was then I started to understand what was going on—like when a ray of light just begins to touch the crests of trees at sunrise, lighting up the tops while the lower part is still in darkness—and I began to realize what we were seeing. What Margene had said about it being a miracle and there being no other way to explain it, came back to me.

"Frieda," I said, "can you get a clean cloth and get it good and wet, then wipe off this dried blood," indicating with my hand the place on her daughter's leg where the bone had been sticking out. She went out to the kitchen and came back several moments later with a white towel in her hands. She was hesitant to touch the wound at first, but after Anita reassured her that it didn't hurt, Frieda gently swabbed off that part of her daughter's leg where the wound had been.

I say, "had been," because it wasn't there anymore. No bone sticking through; no torn skin. I looked closely and saw the tell-tale length of white line marking the spot where the wound had been, just like on my leg. Otherwise there was nothing to indicate what had happened to this little girl that afternoon.

"Do you think we ought to keep the splint on her, just to make sure?" Hugo said. His face was still wreathed in confusion, like a person who has lost their balance and is about to fall over. "Shouldn't we still be trying to get her to the hospital?" he added.

I shook my head. "No, Hugo, I don't think we need to. In fact, let's try taking off this splint. We can do it a little at a time and if she starts to feel pain, we can put it back on again. But I don't think your daughter is going to feel anything hurtful."

How could I tell these good folks what had happened to me back in the fall? I was still dealing with the unreality of my experience, something that was so far out of my normal life understanding that there was no place to put it. It belonged in a place of its own.

We began to loosen the cords around Anita's leg, a little at a time, just like I'd suggested. Frieda was hovering over us and asking her daughter every few moments if her leg was beginning to hurt.

"No, Momma," Anita said. "It hardly hurts at all." Then the little girl would reach out her hand and touch the leg, as if testing the truth of what she'd just said. After we had taken off all of the cords holding the splint onto her leg, we carefully removed the slats of wood from alongside the leg. I looked down at the little girl, a question on my face. But she just shook her head and said that it still felt all right; there was no pain.

"Hugo," I said, "Fred and I are going to drive back to our place now. In the meantime, call Doc Phelps again and have him come out here to check on your daughter once he gets back in. But I think she's going to be all right."

Hugo was still shaking his head and Frieda had her hand pressed against her mouth like people do when they're either afraid or don't know what to say. She was sitting on the sofa beside her daughter, her arm around Anita's waist, holding her close.

Hugo walked out to the truck with us. "I don't know what to say," he said. "I *know* that leg was broken and the bone sticking out when Anita called out for me after she fell. It was broken, Cornell."

"I believe you, Hugo. But sometimes the Good Lord sees fit to change what has happened for the better." I just looked him in the eyes and smiled. I could tell that he was still bewildered and words failed him, just like they had me several months back. Josh jumped up in the truck and we drove off, leaving Hugo looking after us, a stunned look on his face.

Of course Doc Phelps called me later that night, wanting to know "what in the thunderation" was going on and had I seen the little girl's leg broken, like her papa was telling him? Yes, I said and then reminded Doc of a similar incident in the late autumn out at our place. He was silent for a long time, so quiet that I wondered if we'd been disconnected. But he finally spoke up.

"Cornell, if what you and Hugo are telling me is, ah . . . accurate—I'm not saying you aren't telling the truth, understand?—well then, I purely don't know what to make of it. Two miracles in the space of three months are too much for my feeble mind to comprehend. Not withstanding medical science and everything that I've been taught and learned along the way."

He paused for a bit, then continued. "But in science we do have to allow for what some people call miracles. There are gaps in our knowledge and . . . well, you get what I'm saying?"

I told Doc that I understood and that what I'd seen in these two events only made me question myself more as to what I thought which way was up and which way was down. And with that Doc Phelps said goodnight.

The final incident that we experienced when Josh was still with us—well, it wasn't the last thing, but at the time we thought it was—came about when we had driven into town on Thursday to get some hardware we needed for the farm. By this time Josh was a regular in our truck, whether we were going to the fields, a neighbor's, or into town, like we did then.

South Fork is small, just one road running through it, a continuation of the main highway that goes through our region. A group of stores are bunched together on both sides of the road as if huddling for warmth; they're all one-story buildings, the painted store fronts mostly bleached out by the combination of fierce summer heat and sub-zero winter temperatures. Fairbern's Hardware, Lilly's Dress Shop, First State Bank, Merrill's Dining Room—and a half-dozen other stores and shops—have been here for as long as I can remember. Perched on the north end of town is Staley's Feed and Grain that serves our farming community.

I pulled the truck into one of the parking spaces off to one side of Fairbern's and we all got out. Zeke Fairbern didn't mind having dogs in the store as long as they were well behaved, so we brought Josh in with us. I went over to where they had the nails and fasteners, Josh in tow, while Fred ambled over to the counter to ask Zeke about some special hardware we needed. We were in the store for probably ten or fifteen minutes and had got pretty much what we needed when we heard a commotion outside.

Most of the people inside the store were rushing to the front door, so we joined them. The crowd spilled out onto the sidewalk, everyone looking down the street to where a pickup truck was sitting skewed at a funny angle in the middle of the road, its front pointing toward Lilly's Dress Shop on the other side of the street.

People had gathered around something or someone on the roadway, and a man was standing by the pickup bent over, holding his head in his hands. Fred and Josh and me went up to the crowd to see what was going on. Sprawled there on the road was a young boy, maybe eight or nine years old, face down on the pavement.

Several men were around the boy and one was kneeling; it looked like he was taking the boy's pulse. After a minute he shook his head and slowly got to his feet. Meanwhile the man standing by the pickup—I guess he was the driver—started wailing and crying hard. I saw Edna Mae, a woman who went to the same church as us, standing a few feet from me in the crowd. I went over and asked her what had happened.

"That little boy ran out in the street sudden like to get something and the truck came along and hit him. The driver didn't stand a chance to avoid him, he ran out so fast like." She shook her head and looked at the driver. "I sure pity that man, what he must be going through right now."

Meanwhile a lady from one of the stores came out with a sheet and walking over to where the boy lay, spread it over the body so that it was completely covered. I knew then that the boy was dead. Fred was standing not far from me, so I went over to him and said that we should be getting back home; there was nothing we could do here right now.

We walked back to our truck and were ready to get in when I noticed that Josh wasn't with us. I looked around for him, but he wasn't in sight. Then through a gap between some people in the crowd I saw Josh: he had his nose stuck under the sheet and was licking the boy's head. Right about then I heard a murmur rise up from the folks who were still standing around the boy's body, like the sound you hear at a ball game when a player makes a good play.

Right away I knew what he was doing and everything that had happened to me and to Hugo's daughter flashed before my eyes with an irrational clarity, a lightning bolt illuminating the night-darkened landscape of my mind. Fred and I sprinted back over to where the boy was lying on the pavement, except now he wasn't lying down, but sitting up, a dazed look in his eyes. A man and a woman, who I took to be his parents, were hugging him with tears running down their faces, and the driver of the truck was standing next to them, a look on his face like I'd seen on Hugo's several months back: a combination of confusion and relief at what he was witnessing.

I called for Josh and he came over to where we were, looking up at me with that intelligent light in his eyes. But now I knew what was going on. I looked back at the crowd, but they were all looking at the boy, so we got in the truck and drove off.

I didn't say anything for a long time. Fred was looking straight ahead through the windshield, but from time to time he'd glance over at me, trying to gauge what my mood was. Josh sat between us, looking outside at what he could see, seemingly unperturbed by what had just happened back in South Fork. Finally I spoke.

"Son, what do you make of what went on there in town?" I already knew what had happened, but I wanted to see if he did.

"Dad, there's something going on with Josh, isn't it?"

I nodded a yes.

"He has some sort of healing power, doesn't he?"

I nodded again. Fred turned and resumed looking through the windshield and we didn't speak for the rest of the trip back home.

I told Margene about what happened in town, just as I'd told her about what happened with Frieda and Hugo's little girl. She knew right away what it was, and didn't hesitate to say so. That's the way Margene is, honest and direct.

"Cornell, I already told you what I think about it," she said. Her dark eyes were flashing with what some people might misinterpret as impatience, but I knew from experience that it was passion. "That dog has a gift from God, pure and simple. Now don't expect me to tell you why God would give a dog that sort of power, or ability. From what I understand, a gift is just that: something that the person didn't have to begin with and they didn't do anything to earn or deserve. Which means that it's not for us to question or dispute about. It's God's business."

"All right," I said, "I see that. But animals? Tell me where in the Bible God gives an animal the gift to heal people."

"Maybe not heal, but how about Balaam's donkey? He could speak because God gave him the ability to do that. And some people got healed just by touching a cloth that the apostle Paul had on him, or sometimes even if his shadow fell on folks." She looked at me with a triumphant expression. Margene likes to win and is good at that enterprise.

"Okay," I said. "There's no way to prove it one way or another by quoting Bible verses. I guess we'll just have to accept that Josh has some sort of power from God to heal and leave it at that."

"That's fine with me," she said, then got up and went into the kitchen to prepare dinner.

Later that evening we got a telephone call from Doc Phelps. As I expected it was about what had happened in South Fork that day.

"Doc, I think we got another miracle on our hands," I said. "Now, I didn't feel that boy's pulse or see him up close, but the folks that did thought he was dead." I paused and waited for his response.

"Cornell, I heard all that from other people, the ones that were there. But the real reason I called was to warn you about something. There are folks who think that what your dog is doing is wrong. Someone told me they thought it was from the devil. Another person said that it was 'unnatural.' I'm just repeating what I've heard, so don't you go and get all heated up at me about this."

"Doc, that is the most ridiculous thing I've ever heard! Get heated up? Why, it's beyond that. You'd think folks would be grateful if some people are getting healed, not to mention a little boy getting back his life . . . if that's what happened."

"Cornell, you're preaching to the choir. I'm not saying that your dog can heal people. Like I told you, it's beyond my ability to explain this according to what I've learned. All I'm saying is that if I were you I'd keep your dog somewhere inside for a couple of days until all this blows over."

I forced myself to calm down and acknowledge that Doc Phelps was only trying to be helpful. I thanked him and hung up the phone. Then I sat in my chair for a good long while, thinking about what he had said. Why would people get upset if someone was healed? It didn't make sense to me, and I was afraid to share what the doctor had told me with either Margene or Fred. Like he said, it would all blow over in a couple of days.

But just as a precaution, I decided to put Josh inside the barn for the night, along with his parents. I couldn't think of anyone who would want to harm Josh, but you can't predict what people will do when they are worked up about something. Especially if they believe that they're right.

After dinner I spent some extra time with Josh and his folks out in the barn, rubbing him down, petting him, and just sitting around and watching him. He was frolicking about, just like the young dog that he was, exploring different parts of the barn. But occasionally he'd come up to me with those intelligent eyes and look steady at me, like he was trying to communicate something.

Just as a precaution I got out an old padlock and locked up the barn that night. Then I trudged back to the house, ready for bed. I spent a few minutes looking up some things in the old family Bible that my parents had passed down to me. Then Margene and I crawled into bed, ready for a good night's sleep.

I was dreaming about walking down a lonely country road; it was dark, as black as the inside of a tar barrel, but somehow I could make out the dim outlines of things around me. The wind was blowing up a storm and I could hear the creaking of twisted trees limbs above me as they waved wildly in the gale. Leaves and twigs were sailing past me like small missiles borne along on the frantic wind. Suddenly there was the sound of a sharp crack, and a large branch gave way on a tall tree off to my right. Then I woke up, with Margene shaking me.

"Cornell, did you hear that? It sounded like a rifle shot."

"What?" I said, still groggy with sleep and struggling to emerge from my dream world.

"I said that I heard something that sounded like a rifle shot, and it was nearby."

I rolled out of bed and glanced out the window. The sky to the east was light gray, a prelude to the sunrise that would come in about a half hour. I looked down at the barn and saw that the big double doors were standing open, swinging slightly in the early morning breeze.

"What the . . .?" I said to myself. I distinctly remembered putting the big padlock on the doors last night and feeling the solid thud as the shackle slid into the locking mechanism. I pulled on my old jeans and a flannel shirt and padded downstairs, ready to head out for the barn. Fred met me at the bottom of the stairs, his hair standing up every which way after just getting out of bed himself.

"Did you hear that shot, Dad?"

"Yeah, I guess I did. But I'm worried about the barn doors standing wide open. I know I locked them last night."

Fred and I walked out the back of the house, letting the screen door slap against the jamb. It sounded loud in the early morning quiet. The air was cool and fresh, and the slight breeze felt good on my face as we walked toward the barn. It was too early yet for the birds to be up, but we could hear the soft shuffling of our feet as we walked along. The gray skyline was beginning to turn lighter with each passing minute, outlining the sharp peak of the barn roof against the sky.

It was dark inside the barn, but we didn't need a light to see what had happened. Josh's body was lying just inside the barn doors, still and lifeless. His mom and dad were crouched down alongside him, like they were guarding him. But no further harm could come to him now.

Fred went over to where Josh was lying and knelt down beside him. I glanced at the padlock lying on the ground just outside one of the doors, its thick shank cut in two. Someone must have used a large bolt cutter to cut through it like that.

I came over to where Fred was kneeling beside Josh. His face was streaked with tears running down his cheeks, but he wasn't making a sound. The bullet had gone into Josh's chest, right over the place where the heart was.

Whoever did this knew what they were doing and had planned out the crime carefully.

Fred and I stayed there for quite a while next to Josh, taking turns stroking his cooling body and comforting the parents as best we could. Doc Phelps's words of last night came back to me and I inwardly kicked myself for not taking him more seriously. I was not looking forward to telling Margene about this; she had grown as fond of Josh as any animal we'd had over the years.

The rest of that day stayed gray and overcast as heavy clouds from an approaching front moved in. I think that our emotions matched their color. Margene and Fred took it the hardest, not that I didn't. But they seemed to have had a special attachment to the dog and the two spent the rest of the day moping around the house. Later on Fred went out to the barn and found some of the leftover cedar we had bought for the springtime repairs to the house and began making a box in which to bury Josh. I think Fred was comforted by the thought that Josh would like the pleasant smell of the wood and would appreciate the careful work that he was putting into the box. None of us wanted to call it what it was: a coffin.

I called Sheriff Myron about the break-in and shooting, and he said that he'd send a man out the next day to investigate, but practically speaking there was little he could do. I knew that, but it still made me mad that someone could have been so deceived and evil as to have done this awful thing.

After dinner Fred told me that was going to sleep out in the barn, next to the box he'd made. He had crafted the cover out of a beautiful piece of cedar heartwood; Fred had beveled the edges so it would fit snug on top. He and Margene found some satiny kind of fabric to line the box and after Fred had tacked the cloth into place, he gently lowered Josh's body into it. He found seven brass screws we had leftover from another job, and with these he screwed the cover down tight.

I stayed out there with Fred and talked until we both felt sleepy, then I came back to the house for the night. He had hauled out an old sleeping bag and put it on a bed of straw over the rough dirt floor. The momma and papa dogs huddled around him; the box with Josh in it was on an old table right next to them.

Sometime during the night I was awakened by the heavy rumblings of an approaching storm. Soon bright flashes of lightning were coming every few seconds and then the rain hit, drowning out every sound but its own. Thunder shook the house and it seemed like the whole earth around us was shaking with it. I slipped in and out of sleep, but every time I woke up the storm was dominating the universe. I don't know how long it lasted, but eventually I fell into a deep sleep.

Saturday morning was bright and clear; the storm had washed away all impurities from the sky and air, and the trees and bushes were bursting with new green life: spring was coming to our part of the world after a long, dreary winter.

Fred and I drove out to a place in the fields he figured would be a good spot to bury Josh. It was on a little knoll a bit higher than the rest of the surrounding land, looking down on what would be a green meadow by summer. We spent the better part of the morning digging a grave, one deep enough that the weather and any marauding animals wouldn't disturb over the coming years.

"I want to bury him tomorrow," Fred said. "In the morning, just as the sun is coming up. Can we do a sort of ceremony here, instead of going to church?"

"Why sure, son," I told him. Fred had never expressed much interest in religious things before. I think that was the moment when I began to look at him with a different perspective. As a parent it is all too easy to think of your offspring as remaining perennially in the child state, just as you knew him during all those long growing up years. But Fred was rapidly emerging into adulthood, thanks to a mysterious dog that had come into our lives.

The rest of that day was filled with the usual chores around the house and in the pastures; there were always things that needed to be done to get ready for the approaching summer and the additional tasks that season would bring. So we were both ready for an early turn-in to bed that night.

Fred said that he was going to sleep out in the barn again that night. I worried about what effect burying Josh the next day was going to have on him, but we'd have to face that when the time came. Thinking back on his young life I realized this was the first real loss that Fred had experienced.

Like I said, I was real tired and it didn't take me long to get to sleep. The next thing I knew someone was shaking me by the arm, trying to get me awake.

"Dad, Dad. You've got to come out to the barn. Something's happened."

"What's going on? What's happened?" I was so groggy and full of sleep that I couldn't tell where I was for a moment. I tried focusing my eyes in the dim light; Fred was standing by my side of the bed, whispering so as not to wake up Margene.

"Dad, please . . . come out to the barn with me." Fred's voice was urgent, letting me know that he'd brook no hesitation. I got out of bed as quietly as I could and pulled on whatever clothes were handy. The sky was still clear and the air had that transparent milky white look just before the sun comes up. It would be another beautiful day.

Fred and I didn't talk as went out to the barn; I was almost afraid to find out what new tragedy we'd find there. It was dim inside, but not so dark that you couldn't make out the shape of objects. Fred led me over to where Josh's box—I still couldn't bring myself to call it a coffin—stood on the old table.

I looked at it, then at Fred. The top of the box was off, lying alongside it. The seven brass screws were neatly lined up next to it. The box was empty.

"Where's Josh, son?"

"I don't know, Dad. That's why I wanted you to come out here. I haven't touched the box since Friday night when I put the top on and screwed in those screws real tight. That cover was on it last night when I went to sleep, but when I woke up this morning, early, it was just like this." Fred gestured with his arm toward the box, the cover, and the screws.

"And another thing." He looked around the inside of the barn, then back at me. "The other two dogs, the momma and the papa, they're gone too."

I didn't say anything, but walked over to where the box was lying on the table. There was nothing in it, just like Fred had said. There wasn't even any dog hair stuck in the fabric. I picked up one of the brass screws and looked at it. I don't know what I expected to see; there were no marks on the head or burred pieces of metal sticking out like you'd expect if someone had bore down real hard with a screwdriver to get the screw out.

"And Dad, another thing." Fred was standing next to me, an intent look in his eyes. "I barred the doors from inside with that four-by-four last night, just like I did the night before." I saw the long square piece of wood he was referring to leaning up against the side of the barn by one of the doors. Fred had put that board through the U-shaped pieces of metal on the inside of the barn doors to hold them closed and prevent anyone from opening the doors from the outside. They could only be opened from within. "No one came in last night," he said. "I was the only person here."

We spent a few more minutes looking around the inside of the barn, trying to find an explanation for what had happened. Of course we didn't find anything; I was hoping that we wouldn't. This was the last incident, the one I referred to earlier, after the boy who had been hit by the truck came back to life.

Margene was the only one of us who didn't seem perturbed by all that had gone on since Josh came to us. Typical of who she was, she had her own answer for this.

"Josh was all about life," she said. "Everything he touched he brought life to, either new life or renewed life. For me, Josh was simply used by God to remind us about who He is."

We never found out who it was that shot him, and I don't care to know. Fred and I drove out later that day to the place in the fields where we had dug his grave. Fred brought along the box he'd made, but he left it empty, except at the last minute he pulled a folded up piece of paper out of his jacket pocket and put it inside the box. Then he screwed on the lid with the brass screws and

Whole Cloth

lowered it into the hole. When we shoveled the rich dark soil into the open grave it made a hollow sound as hit the box.

Journal of the Plague Year

It began on Thursday, about five o'clock in the afternoon. I remember this because it was August 22nd, the Feast Day of Saint Bartholomew and we had just returned home after mass at Sant' Agostino. Claudia turns and looks at me: "You don't look well. What's the matter?"

In the twenty-three years we've been married, Claudia has always been direct. That's what first attracted me to her, back when we were students together at Fra' Stefano's, and then later at the university.

People say that I am somewhat shy and reserved. Yes, I admit it, particularly when it comes to dealing with the gray areas that make up the baffling landscape of relationships. For instance, are people sad . . . and why? Do I detect reluctance in someone to talk . . . and for what reason? But I never ask. I'm too reticent—some would say afraid—to ask. But not Claudia.

She puts her hands on my shoulders and turns me so that we face each other. "Carlo, you look worried. What's wrong?"

When she does this, looks into my eyes, it's like she's looking into a pool of clear water, seeing everything at the bottom, every detail, discerning the pattern of pebbles in the nestling sand that forms the stream bed. But that bothers me, her eyes looking at something inside my soul that I am not willing to examine myself. Not yet.

But I don't say anything, preferring to brush it aside, telling her that I don't know. It's nothing, waving my hand in depreciation, minimizing the importance, all the while reluctant to meet her eyes.

165

She sighs, a long, slow outflow of breath she uses to say things without words. "Why are you like this, Carlo," or something to that effect. She knows me well, Claudia. But she is a good wife, and doesn't push. She knows me.

It is my turn to sigh as I turn away from her and walk into the room that is my study, a place for my books—my many books—and also a place for me to think. Solid boundaries, four walls: rough plaster walls, but there is an artisan's touch in the roughness, a pleasing grainy texture you can feel under your fingertips. A place apart, a space, a refuge from the way life pulls us along like a horse at gallop, headstrong and uncontrollable, heading purposefully back to the place it knows as home. But it is necessary to slow down in life, to somehow tame the willful horse. But our society has done this: put us on the horse speeding home.

What *is* the matter? There was a momentary dizziness, a lightheadedness. Something in the chest, just a touch, but deep. Even now, just thinking about it brings back that feeling, like a shadow suddenly darting out from behind a wall. But more than that, much more.

"Papa?"

I turn away from the wall at the sound of her voice. My beloved Nicola, standing in the doorway, a look of hesitancy and questioning formed on her pale slender face. Beautiful, my Nicola; just like her mother, thank God. Not my looks.

"What, my dove?" She flushes when I say this, as with all my pet names for her. But she also smiles, a little upturn of her mouth at the corners, enjoying my compliment. Her russet eyes show this also, a reflection of her soul. I hope that she knows it's because I love her so much. God didn't see fit to give Claudia and me a son, but I wouldn't trade my dear *piccola colomba*, my little dove, for any son in Italy. I've told her this, fearing that Nicola might regret the lack of a male heir in our family. I don't want her worrying, taking on a false responsibility just because she wasn't born a boy.

"Mama has some soup for us. She wants to know if you'll come?"

Am I ready for an intimate trio in the dining room, where undoubtedly Claudia will once again fix her eyes on me and her face will express a worried concern, accompanied by an occasional sigh? I think not. But I don't want to miss an opportunity to be with my little dove, my lovely daughter. So I nod a "yes," then linger for a few more moments in the study, letting the last drops of obscure, dark shadows leak out of my soul. I finger the rough-textured wall, as if the minute ridges and valleys in the plaster hold the secret of what moves in the concealed recesses of my heart.

Later that evening after the soup—accompanied by our smoky Tuscan cheese and grainy peasant's bread from the *paneria* down the street—Claudia and I sit together on the side of our bed. She strokes my back with soft sympathetic movements. Nicola has left to join a group of young people meeting at the church, something she's become interested in the past several months. It's good that she's there; it's a safe place, the church.

I feel better now, since we had our little supper together. It's like the cloud that hovered over my head earlier in the day has lifted, evaporating under the warmth of familial sunlight. But I still feel traces of its effects lingering inside me, leaving me with a sensation of slight instability, like a person who has just risen from his sick bed after a period of illness.

Finally Claudia breaks the tranquility of the moment. "I'm worried about Nicola."

Yet another concern of hers. She pauses, waiting for my reply.

"Nicola? She's fine. What are you worried about?"

Another sigh, but this time, a short impatient one. "Carlo, how can you not see? How old is our daughter?" Claudia looks at me with expectation filling her eyes, as if my answer will reveal the problem, its inherent truth, and thus her concern.

"She's twenty, of course. And what—?"

"Yes, twenty. And not married!"

So that's it. The concern of a mother that the life of her daughter should accord with her own wishes, leading always to happiness. Still, twenty is twenty, and these days that's beyond the age when a woman should not be without a husband.

"So, she's not seeing anyone?" I already know the answer.

"You know she's not. Since Gian Mario, no one." Now Claudia looks sad, thereby assigning, in her mind, Nicola to the doom of spending the rest of her days alone, an aging spinster in our society, one that puts great value on matrimony and bearing children.

"But Love, she's young yet, a child." I reach over and take her hand and pat it. She looks dour, not wanting to be cheered up by a husband who discounts so much in life. "Give her time. Many of the young men have asked to visit, but Nicola doesn't want to see them. Why, I don't know. But give her time." More pats of my hand.

"Ah, this new age." Claudia breathes out another of her long sighs, seemingly without end this time. "It was simpler when we were young, wasn't it?" She looks up to my face for affirmation. I nod.

"We didn't even know one another. Not until Fra' Stefano. But our parents knew; they made a wise choice." She smiles as she says this. "And it's worked, hasn't it, Carlo? It's worked."

She is still seeking my reassurance, but now it's easy for me to give. Of course it's worked; more than that, it's been like a gift to me, one I could never have chosen for myself. Yes, our parents were wise. We owe a great debt of gratitude to them.

"Listen, Claudia. She doesn't lack for ability and gifts; you know that. She's beautiful. Someone has his eye on her, I'll bet you that." I nod and smile in hopes of encouraging her.

Will my smile work? There's something about dourness that makes it hard for a person to let go of. It wants to plant itself in their hearts, to grow and develop, molding itself into their character until they look and act like it, and finally become it.

Claudia forces herself to give me a wan smile, half-hearted, but there's no spirit behind it. She is worried, depressed about our only child, and I know there is nothing that I can say or do that will help in this matter. It's Claudia's duty as a mother to worry.

That night I awaken from a sound sleep to terror.

All at once I am aware that something terrible has happened, or it is about to happen. Either way it is horrible, unimaginable. I cannot breathe, so I sit up in bed, sweat on my forehead and my heart racing. I think it must beat so loud that Claudia hears it. But she doesn't move; her form underneath the covers is still, sleeping the sleep of the virtuous.

What is it? What is going on? I listen intently for any sound in our house, but there is a terrible roaring in my ears like that of the sea, engulfing all, making it difficult to hear beyond it. Has someone come in unannounced? My thoughts go immediately to Nicola. Where is she? Is she safe? But of course: she is in bed also, safely home at ten o'clock that night. I have seen her, kissed her goodnight.

I try to lie down again, but as soon as my head touches the pillow, a feeling of unutterable fear comes. I can't breathe. It's impossible to lie down, the dread is too great. So I sit back up, only then aware that my hands are gripping the bedclothes as a drowning man would a lifeline, hanging onto it for salvation from the dark fate of the sea. I try to unclench my hands, but it is difficult. They have become stiff. Why do I have to hold so tightly?

I reach over with care and rest my hand on the form of my sleeping wife, my Claudia, underneath the bedclothes. I let my hand touch her softly. I don't want to wake my wife, but I need the tactile assurance that she is there, someone through whom I can connect with a place in the world that is safe. It is very unsafe right now, the darkness, the quiet. The silence is not good, because anything can come of out the quiet, can't it?

Little by little the inner darkness fades, coinciding with the arrival of dawn. My heart stops racing and slows down. The blackness outside becomes less opaque, a dark gray, but penetrable, the forerunner of coming light. There is somehow a feeling of hope in that grayness, because I know it will soon transform itself into day; the sunshine will reestablish familiar shapes and forms. Then it will be safe.

Still I dare not lie back down, even though I begin to shiver in the early morning cold. The sweat on my forehead has dried, and it now feels clammy. But I don't lie down, because it's safer this way. Perhaps if I can prop my head up higher on the pillow, then I can recline a little—not lying down, mind you, but just enough to get back under the covers.

Dio mio, what is this which happens to me? And why? The world has now become a hostile and perilous place; I can't trust it anymore. I stare at the slow transformation of darkness into light, my mind a maze of thoughts that lead nowhere.

All of a sudden Claudia is shaking me: "Wake up, Carlo. Wake up, you sleepyhead! Are you going to sleep away the morning?"

"What is it?" I mumble, wondering why my wife is waking me from a sound sleep. What is wrong? What has possessed her? I blink and squeeze my eyes closed against the dazzling light coming through our bedroom windows.

"'What is it?' you say. It's late—practically midmorning! Are you going to sleep all day, Carlo?"

Claudia bends low over me, putting her face close to mine and peering into my eyes, as if she is seeking the cause for my oversleeping. I feel groggy, like I've taken a potion of sleeping herbs.

All that day the bleary feeling stays with me, hovering in the background of my mind like the fog hanging over distant Colline Metallifere in winter. It mutes everything that I see or say or think. It's like I'm in a perpetual state of not being fully awake, groping with tentative gestures, uncertain and befuddled.

The next night—and then all the succeeding nights—the same thing happens: the fear—stark terror, really—wakes me in the early hours of the morning. But unlike the first time, I can no longer get back to sleep because of the intense emotions grabbing me by the throat. So I arise from my bed with quiet, stealthy movements and find my way into the hallway, careful to not wake my sleeping Claudia.

By putting my hand on the wall for guidance I can tread with hesitating footsteps along the corridor, trying to regain my breath, bent over like the aged, the infirm. I pace this way for some time, trembling from a deep place inside me. For how long I cannot say. When the first signs of gray appear in the eastern sky, I go back to bed for a short time, until Claudia wakes and arises. I arise with her, pretending to have slept all night. I try to convince myself that this is all right, something I can deal with, but I remain numb and tired throughout the day.

Eventually, after many days, then weeks—months perhaps—Claudia notices my languor and seizes on it like a mastiff lunging after a choice morsel tossed from the scullery table. "Carlo," she exclaims, "Now you *have* to tell me! What is happening with you?" There is a sound of panic in her voice, something that I've not heard before. For emphasis, she places her hands on top of my shoulders and squeezes hard. I wince with the pressure.

"I don't know, *Caro*, I don't know!" I am almost pleading under the weight of emotion I am experiencing, one that presses me down with a relentless heaviness. "This is making me crazy; I don't know why this is happening."

Claudia lowers her head toward me and pushes me back, her arms still on my shoulders, until her face is level with mine. Her brown eyes bore into mine as she tries to penetrate the depths of my soul with her gaze. But this time the waters are not clear and limpid; they are swirling and muddy. She cannot discern, and this frustrates her. But more than the anger, I see fear in her eyes.

"Carlo, this cannot go on." She pronounces this with all the gravity of a magisterial edict. But then I see a change in her eyes that I've not seen before—ever. It's the look of defeat. Claudia doesn't know how to cope with this new situation that has come into her life and is turning it upside down. Her eyes become moist, then liquid, as tears begin to roll down her plump cheeks. With a moan she falls forward against me, and together we weep as we clutch one another in an embrace driven by the desperation of the hopeless.

There comes a time during this period—I cannot mark the exact moment it occurs—that the terror begins to take on a shape, a human one. I begin to dream at night, or more exactly, I remember the dreams when I am startled awake in the middle of the night. And what comes to me is the face of Bartolomeo, the uncle who raised me after the death of my mother. He appears in the dreams in the guise of an evil personage, dressed in garments of foreboding and malice. I see his features distorted by a menacing glare, then I awake with an icy grip upon my heart, the pincers of fear squeezing hope and life from me.

The days continue one after another in much this same way, advancing like soldiers in endless procession. I lose track of times and seasons, although they unfold as always. But I am a bystander, not a participant, watching from afar the progress of time in others' lives, but not mine. My appetite wanes, diminishing like the day's breeze as night approaches, and I begin to lose weight, something noticeable to everyone I meet.

"Carlo," they say, "What sort of diet are you on—you of all people, who cannot afford to lose weight!" They say this with a smile, but their eyes drift up to my haggard face, remarking the weary visage, the sagging flesh—the spiteful offspring of sleepless nights. I am tired beyond measure.

And something else happens: I become fearful to venture outside the house into the streets and lanes I've known since boyhood. There is a sinister feel to them now, and I dread the trips I must make to accompany Claudia on her visits to the market or to our friends. There is something inside me that wants to recoil in the face of the overwhelming feeling of anxiety that accompanies travel outside the safe boundaries of our house. I want to huddle in one of its sheltering corners, still miserable, but knowing that my life in this haven is manageable.

Nicola notices, too. But she's like her father, saying nothing, just observing in silence. Her eyes take in my figure with a quick glance, but her face doesn't change except for a fleeting shadow that drifts across her light brown eyes, then moves on. But I see that Nicola is spending more time with me now, making excuses to be in the same room as I, pretending to look for a book or wanting to rest a few moments with me in my study while I work on the manuscripts.

Finally, she speaks.

"Papa, can I tell you about something?"

Her face undergoes subtle changes, taking on a different appearance, as though a light is shining from within her. She is smiling—a look of pleasure, of delight. My mind leaps forward and grasps at an answer, too impatient to wait for her to disclose it. She has met someone new, one who pleases her and now she wants to describe him to me.

"Papa, you know I've been going to the Duomo often these past weeks?"

She is referring to our beautiful cathedral, the Duomo di Siena, now over a hundred and seventy-five years old. We residents of the city are very proud of our cathedral. I was baptized there as a child and took my instruction in the faith under Fr. Pisano within those holy walls.

I nod in agreement with Nicola, but am wondering where she is taking me in her story. Has she met a young man pleasing to her at church? I look at her, a question mark on my face as I wait for her to continue.

"My friend, Caterina, and I have been going there to hear a most remarkable preacher. Almost all of my friends are going to the Duomo to hear him; he's been speaking every night now for two weeks!"

Nicola waits for me to register surprise or pleasure at this news; instead I feel my facial muscles form to show disappointment. What? No new young man, no betrothal in her future? See how foolish we parents can be? I have picked up Claudia's anxiety for our only child, projecting onto our daughter the unspoken fate of an aging spinster still living with her parents as we advance into senility.

Her features darken in concern for me, for my lack of a proper (in her eyes) response to her youthful enthusiasm. Then it passes and she leans forward again. Nicola, for all her likeness to me, has learned how to plow the fields of relationships, looking for greater harvests that she knows are certain to be reaped there.

"Oh Papa, will you come with me to hear him? Perhaps tonight?"

Now she is smiling, the delight of a daughter inviting her father to an important event. I know at once that I must not disappoint her in this, even though every particle of my being wants to run and hide. Going out? To the Duomo to hear a strange preacher? Why would anyone in his right mind want to do such a thing? Particularly someone who is battling daily forces of darkness within himself that are beyond comprehension or explanation?

I smile back at her, an act of my will power—such as it is—because I know from some deep place in my father's heart I cannot refuse this opportunity to be with *mia piccola colomba,* my little dove. Yet I tremble within.

"Yes, my dove, we will go this evening."

And thus, unbeknownst to me, I enter into a new phase of my life. It's an unfamiliar territory that has been waiting many years to be discovered, to be revealed to me. But at the moment I am unaware of this; it is something that is coming, but not yet here. I am like a blind man who can only perceive that which lies under his fingertips, a prisoner of finite space.

We go, my little dove and I, as the lowering evening settles over our city and quiet comes to our streets. The lamplighters are illumining the lanterns hanging from the tall iron poles that grace the *piazza* in the center of Siena, creating yellow circles of light on the rough stone street. It is strange, the way darkness has of transforming the familiar into the unknown.

The profile of the Duomo is recognizable from a distance as we walk together—Nicola's friends have joined us by prearrangement—gracing the dimly lit horizon. The tall bell tower, impressive with its alternating horizontal layers of white and green-black marble, stands out above the rest of the imposing structure.

Nicola is animated and chatting with her friends, a side of her I've not seen before; at home she is so quiet and subdued. She links arms with her good friend, Caterina, and their heads almost touch as they bend toward one another, sharing excited confidences. Several young men—some of whom I know from their occasional visits to Nicola at our house, but others who are strangers to me—gather at the edges of our little group, stealing covetous glances at my little dove as we progress toward the cathedral.

Despite our casual pace, I feel breathless at times, and a strange disquiet stirs within me. I fight with the fear, all for Nicola's sake, vowing to not let her see me at my worst. Carlo the Tranquil, the Quiet One—that is how my friends and acquaintances perceive me, and that is how I want my family to know me. I am shivering in the early night air, even though a temperate spring is well advanced in our region.

Nicola and Caterina lead our small procession to the front of the cathedral; we enter through a small wooden door inset in one of the three massive portals. I am surprised to see so many people approaching the church; so many, in fact, that we have to wait our turn to enter. Women reach into their cloaks and bring out shawls and scarves with which to cover their heads out of respect once inside the sacred building.

At last we enter and pass by the Holy Water stoups. I dip my fingers into the cool water, tracing a pattern, the sign of the Cross, on my forehead. I've done this since childhood, but tonight I feel myself reflecting on what this means. It is ritual, yes, but symbolism is now transforming itself into reality, an understanding that keeps a teasing distance just beyond the fingertips of my reason. Nicola turns back toward me, interrupting my thoughts, making sure that I am well. Tonight she is my parent; I am the child, following in obedience.

I force myself to smile at her, but my stomach feels bound in knots, almost painful. She smiles back, a gentle gesture, and at that moment I see my little dove transformed with a kind of radiant beauty, a glow that seems to encircle her face. I shake my head, thinking that I have gone into a trance, a vision. But I recognize that this is no vision: everything around me—the people, the stone walls of the edifice—are real. Something out of the ordinary is happening, but strangely for once, I feel no fear or apprehension.

There is a subdued murmur, the sound of many hundreds of people within the church. It echoes off the vast cathedral ceiling far above us—I see now how many have already entered before us—and we are enveloped in the sound falling around us like a soft woven garment.

"Papa, we'll sit here."

Nicola has led us to the front of the seating area, just to the right of the beautiful elevated pulpit. She points in an authoritative way with her arm, indicating where we will sit, and I, the obedient child, wordlessly follow and take my seat beside her. I turn toward her, still enthralled by the beautiful glow coming from my dove. Who is this preacher, I ask *sotto voce*.

"His name is Bernardino," she replies. "He comes from Massa Marittima, but he has preached all over the country."

I start to ask another question, but we are interrupted by the entrance of the priests. The throng of people—some are yet entering the cathedral—rise to their feet. One of the priests (I do not recognize him, he is a younger man) leads the congregation in the *vespro*, the Evening Prayers. I am surprised at the ease with which Nicola follows the service; we didn't take her to church that often when she was growing up, yet she acts as though she's always worshipped this way. It seems so natural for her.

After a while the prayers draw to a close, and a priest I hadn't noticed before (he had been standing back from the others) comes forward and mounts the pulpit stairs with a slow methodical purpose. He is of medium height and thin of frame. His beard, flecked with gray, forms a fringe around his face. He wears a simple brown hooded robe, tied at the waist with a plain cord. A country priest, I think to myself.

"That's him," Nicola whispers in quiet excitement. I turn to look at her and her face is still radiant with light, a rapturous smile on her lips, her eyes focused on the simple priest. From the pulpit he motions the people to be seated, but my little dove seems caught up in another world, staring at Bernardino and forgetting to sit. I pull at her sleeve, and like someone in the midst of a dream she lowers herself to the rough wooden bench.

Before the priest speaks he positions a rectangular wooden plaque in front of him in the pulpit. The letters I. H. S. are inscribed, or perhaps painted, on the board. Nicola nudges me and whispers, "That's the Holy Name of Jesus," nodding toward the plaque. Then Bernardino begins to speak and I am surprised by the force of his voice, or rather, its intensity. He is not shouting, but his words come forth in a way that captures everyone's attention.

Although I am concentrating on listening, I cannot now recall a single word he uttered. It is as though I am entering a world apart, although I am physically present in this one, sitting with Nicola on the hard wooden bench in the Duomo.

It is only after Bernardino finishes speaking that I realize I am feeling at peace, a blessed calm that is devoid of anxiety or worry. The knot in my stomach has gone. The darkness that has surrounded my heart for so long has given way to light. I feel normal, the way my life used to be before all this began.

After the officiating priest gives the blessing many begin to file out of the cathedral, but clusters of people remain in small groups, talking among themselves. There is a different feeling here tonight from what I remember when we have attended the Sunday mass. Nicola turns in the direction of the priest, Bernardino, and walks straight toward him. I want to tell her not to disturb the holy man, reverting to the protective parent cautioning a headstrong child. It's too late, she is already approaching him.

Bernardino sees Nicola and smiles. Although he appears physically frail and his face—now that I am seeing him at closer vantage—is lined and aged, when he smiles he is wreathed in beauty. Nicola—I am fearful of her forwardness—kneels before the priest and he places his hand on her head, intoning a short prayer as he does. Then Bernardino extends his hand to my daughter and bids her rise.

I stand at a distance transfixed. Am I seeing a play, is this a sort of enactment, rather than real life? How is it possible that my little dove, my sweet, tender Nicola, can be standing in this holy man's presence with such ease and self-confidence?

Nicola turns to me and motions with her hand that I come join her. I am hesitant, for all of a sudden familiar fears begin to surface: risking the disapproval of others, making a mistake in the presence of someone of in authority. I feel awkward, like a child, as though I am ten years old. But at last my feet begin to move and I approach Bernardino and my daughter.

"Father Bernardino," she says, "This is my *papa*." Nicola holds out her hand and takes mine as we turn to face the priest. I am at a loss as to what to say, and my hesitancy must show on my face. But Bernardino just smiles and reaches out his arm toward me. I start to grasp his hand in a traditional greeting, but instantly see I am mistaken, for the priest places his hand on my head and prays a blessing over me. I bow my head in acknowledgment.

What happens next is difficult for me to relate, let alone understand. Yet, I will endeavor to explain it. Without any warning or premonition, a sensation of tingling passes down my body, starting at my head and continuing to my feet. It is not disagreeable, but it is disturbing, like biting into an apple and instead of tasting the familiar sweetness, experiencing the tart sharpness of an orange. The feeling is momentary and brief, passing almost as soon as it began, leaving me somewhat shocked, if that is the word to use.

No . . . surprised.

I blink my eyes in confusion, attempting to reorient myself to the world I have known for my forty-one years here on this earth. The priest looks at me keenly, but with a gentle smile on his lips. He moves his hand to rest on my shoulder.

"My son, I see that you carry great pain within you."

My mind refuses to work, to think: it is blank. My feet feel rooted to the spot as though I were one of the marble statues that adorn the interior of the Duomo. Bernardino continues speaking to me, but I find that my attention is drawn to his eyes: they are a light gray, matching his beard.

"You have carried this pain for a long time, my son, and now the Lord says it is time to take this burden from you, to give it to Him." There is also something else in his eyes; it is kindness. I've have never seen such a look of profound kindness before.

I nod in agreement without really understanding the import of his words, but I somehow know they carry the weight of truth. My heart also knows this and I feel a desperate stirring of hope within me that I've not felt for many years. Yes, many years.

Father Bernardino takes his hand from my shoulder and turns to Nicola for a moment, then back to me, including us both. "Please come and see me tomorrow before mid-day. I will be in my rooms in the Friary. Come then." His eyes have an intensity of regard as he looks at me; he nods, then walks away, accompanied by the retinue of priests from the Duomo. Nicola, by my side, bows her knee in a quick *riverenza* as he leaves, then looks at me.

"Papa, how do you feel?" She is looking at me closely, but with kindness. Not critically. She is smiling and she looks beautiful. *Mia piccola colomba.*

It takes me a few moments before I am able to give life to the words that come in my mind. They arise like the silent puffy white clouds that mysteriously form above the distant western mountain ridge.

"Peace. Yes . . . I feel peace."

Nicola smiles and together we walk arm in arm toward the rear of the Duomo. By now most of the people have left. When we go through the great wooden door into the night, I am startled to see a large conflagration off to my left: yellow flames are reaching into the black night, illuminating the piazza. I think that a house has caught fire, but there is no panic or sense of urgency among the onlookers standing around the fire.

"Look, Papa: it's a *falo delle vanita*: people are throwing their valuables, their 'vanities'—the things they've worshipped instead of the Lord—into the fire." We turn to watch the blaze rise higher as people approach and throw in books, clothes, even jewelry. "Father Bernardino preaches about these things," she says, "but he never makes people get rid of them. Only if they want to—if they feel the conviction of the Lord in their hearts."

I turn again to stare at my daughter, my little dove. Who is this beautiful young girl who has become such a wise young woman? Is this the Nicola I have known all of my life? I am beginning to wonder, but I say nothing to her. This is a night of surprises, and at the same time, of mysteries.

We stand by the bonfire for a few minutes, and Nicola talks with Caterina and her other friends. The orange-red light illuminates our faces and casts tall wavering shadows on the sides of the nearby buildings as the flames mount up and then subside in a rhythm like that of the ocean. After several minutes we bid goodnight to her friends and start for home, always arm in arm, my little dove leaning against me as we walk.

"Papa, can I ask you something?" Nicola turns her face up toward mine, her eyes intent and serious.

After I nod my assent, she continues. "Father Bernardino talked about the pain inside you. Papa, he said you are carrying a burden. What does he mean?"

This is something I have put off discussing with Nicola, or anyone, thinking that there will be a time—some time in the future—that will be the right moment to open up my soul. I have kept postponing that time, and it has never come—until now.

I struggle with what to say and how to say it. I would rather continue in my comfortable ritual of avoidance, to not say anything, but somehow I know that I must now break that practice. This is the time to speak; it's not the time of my own choosing, and this knowledge is what works so furiously against my heart. I sigh, and begin.

"You know, Nicola, that my mother—your grandmother—died when I was very young." I sigh again, then take another breath, despite the ache in my chest that makes me feel as if I have leather bands tightening around me. "I don't remember that—her dying, I mean. I just recall being taken to a place away from where we had lived, somewhere that felt different and not safe. That was where my *zio*, my uncle Bartolomeo, lived with his wife, Aunt Francesca."

We are walking away from the center of town now, entering the familiar narrow streets of our quarter. It is dark, but we know the way; we don't need light. Nicola squeezes my arm from time to time, encouraging me as I talk.

"I can only guess that my father was overcome with grief at the loss of his wife, that he didn't have the strength to take care of me. So all I can remember is being with them, my uncle and aunt—a childless couple. I guess that's why they took me in, but somehow I knew that they weren't my real parents. No one told me, not back then, but I knew they weren't my father and mother."

I tell her how uncle Bartolomeo never smiled, a tired, weary man, never looking at me. Thus, I thought myself as being in the way, and that I somehow displeased him. My aunt at least tried to make me feel a part of their household, but I don't think that she really knew how to do this. Looking back now, I think she was intimidated by her husband, by the force of his character. So from the very first I have always felt guilty about myself, of who I am. I thought that I was an intruder in their lives, but more than that, an intruder into the world. But not knowing why. It felt confusing to me, and I always assumed it was somehow my fault.

"Then came his anger," I tell Nicola, glancing at her face, not able to discern her expression in the dark that surrounds us as we make our way down the cobblestone streets. But I can sense her silent expression of concern, the tightening of her hand on my arm. "Uncle Bartolomeo was an angry man, and he eventually took out that anger on me. But that wasn't all; there was more than the beatings and punching."

I pause, unable to know how to convey that which is unspeakable, particularly to my little dove, my Nicola, so innocent and childlike. How can I tell her about the night when zio Bartolomeo came home drunk when I was already in bed, of being awakened with his sour breath on my face and his greedy hands on my body? And then the innumerable nights of terror and shame that followed. It is from this time that a malignancy began to grow within me and took root in my soul; it grew in the darkness of shame and silence. So I don't talk about that with her. This is enough for now.

We reach our house and Nicola pulls me to a stop just before we enter the door, turning to face me. "Papa, I love you so much!" she says, and throws her arms around me. I am caught off guard by her spontaneous gesture, and I only manage to put one arm around my daughter, the other pinned to my side by her embrace. Nicola hangs on to me like a novice swimmer who is caught in strong currents and hangs on to the seasoned swimmer for her very life. But it is Nicola who I feel is pouring her life into me, a struggling man caught in a powerful tide of emotions and memories that threaten to pull him far from shore and submerge him under the dark waters of pain.

That night I sleep better, but disturbing dreams come in the quiet hours of the early morning: images of hideous creatures—stealthy animals that creep on the ground with human-like faces, one of them like *zio* Bartolomeo. But I don't wake up with the heart-stopping terror of the many past nights, and for that I am grateful.

Morning dawns, the sky aflame with a beautiful sunrise that I watch from my bed, a painting that displays spectacular colors from a celestial palette. Claudia sleeps with the peace of the righteous beside me, unmindful of the masterpiece to which I am a grateful witness. My mind fills with questions, but ones that have no answer. I admit to a feeling of anxiety about seeing Father Bernardino today, not knowing what to expect from our meeting. What is the fascination that Nicola has with this person, even if he is a "holy man"? And why did I agree to see him today? After all, I could have made an excuse to avoid our meeting. But now it is too late, so I sigh, and arise with care from the bed, so as not to disturb my still-sleeping wife.

"Good morning, Papa!" Nicola greets me in the kitchen with a brilliant smile that rivals the sunlight streaming through the open window. We sit at the small table and drink our *caffe*, hardly speaking. Nicola is occupied reading a small booklet, scarcely touching her food.

"Oh, sorry Papa," she says when I point out that her *caffe* is growing cold. She holds up the small booklet for me to see. "It's a collection of Father Bernardino's writings," she says, her expression animated and full of energy. "He explains things so clearly," she continues, "he has so much wisdom— from the Lord, of course. We are so blessed to have him with us now." She looks to me for approval, and I don't know how to respond. So I give a noncommittal nod.

I have grown up in the church, as did all of my friends, receiving instruction from our parish priests and nuns; I took my first communion, and was baptized into the Body of Christ when I was still quite young. I believe in God, but Nicola talks about Him in a way that conveys she knows *more*, or has a special understanding. I don't know; it is puzzling. When I think about this I feel like a child, without knowledge of things that lie outside my little world. I shouldn't be worried, but I must admit to having some anxieties about this Father Bernardino and his teachings. This is why I sense the creeping tendrils of disquietude about seeing him today growing inside me.

But Nicola's cheerfulness pulls me along and she doesn't allow me to have much time to think about, or worry over, my fears. Yes—there it is. I have named it: fears. That's what they are, but if you ask me why, I have no answer for you. If I look at my life—the surface part that others see, the appearance of things that surround me—I see no reason to have fears, or at the least, anxieties, about what is happening.

Yet I do, I cannot deny this. But I make the decision to not let them spoil the time I have with my little dove.

"Ready, Papa?"

"Yes, *mia cara*." I answer with a brave expression and put a smile on my face as we set out together toward the friary and my appointment with the "holy man." The loveliness of the day compels me to believe that all will be well. Nicola's arm is linked through mine as we walk at a leisurely pace along the *vicolo*, the narrow alley, in the direction of the *piazza del Campo*. Her closeness adds to my feeling of hope that all, indeed, will be well.

The morning sun has not yet risen high in the immaculate blue sky, and the early light creates deep shadows along the high walls of the buildings that border the *vicolo*. As we walk toward the *piazza* I experience a curious vision: the alleyway is shrouded in somber shadows, but the open *piazza* before us is bathed in sunshine. I have the strange impression of walking down a dark tunnel toward light, one that is full of undefined promise. Because my little dove is holding onto my arm, I let that promise penetrate my heart and plant seeds of hopeful expectations.

The friary where Father Bernardino stays is close by the Duomo and our path takes us alongside that imposing structure. Nicola points out the remains of last night's *falo*, the bonfire into which people threw their prized possessions. All that remains now is a heap of dark gray ashes on the stones of the street. I think about how fire can consume that which we hold so important and valuable to us, like the "vanities" thrown last night into the blaze. And now nothing remains save a pile of cold, dirty ashes.

One of the brothers answers the door at the friary, and we announce our presence. They seem to know Nicola here, and everyone smiles as we enter. A nun, an older woman with a small wooden cross hanging by a woven cord from her neck and dressed in a plain black dress, approaches. She smiles as she greets Nicola; again, it seems that everyone here knows my daughter.

"Father Bernardino will be with you shortly," the brother tells us, and invites us to take a seat on the wooden bench in the hall. Nicola stays to talk with the nun, while I sit. They speak with heads bowed towards one another; the nun says something to Nicola, who nods her head in agreement every now and then, but I cannot hear much of what they say. My eyes take in the hallway: there are no decorations on the white plaster walls save for a large crucifix at the end of the hall. A door opposite to where I am sitting begins to open and Father Bernardino emerges. He looks at me and smiles. I get to my feet in a hurry, rather awkwardly, and start to bow, but he holds out an admonitory hand.

"No, *signore*, please—that is not necessary."

He puts both arms around me, taking me by surprise, and gives a gentle embrace, kissing me on the cheek as he does so. If the heat I feel suffusing my face is any indication, I am flushing deeply. Father Bernardino turns to greet Nicola, who sinks to one knee before him in a graceful *riverenza*. As he did the night before, the priest places his small hand on her hair and intones a short blessing. He then embraces her, as he did me. Nicola is radiant, and speaks several hurried words to the Father before stepping back.

"Let us go into this room," Father Bernardino says to me, indicating the place from where he has just come. I see through the half-opened door a medium-sized room, with books lining the shelves on one plain plaster wall. It is simple and bereft of ornamentation, with the exception of a beautiful metal cross, perhaps silver, on the wall. The sunlight coming through the window reflects off it, illumining the room with a gentle gleaming luster.

As I turn to follow the Father I feel someone touch me on the shoulder from behind. It is Nicola; she is holding out her arms to me, inviting an embrace. Tears are shimmering in her dark eyes, taking me unawares. What is she feeling? I am paralyzed in this moment by the suddenness of my daughter's actions, so unexpected—this, my *piccola colomba*, my once-shy child.

"Oh, Papa," she says as we hold one another in a tight embrace. "I will be praying for you!" She pulls back and holds me at arm's length, looking at me through a tender veil of tears, like a parent looks at her beloved child, so proud. Once again I am the child and Nicola has become the parent. Then I turn and enter the room with Father Bernardino.

Afterward, Nicola is waiting for me in the foyer as the priest and I exit the room. I have no idea how long we have been in there, but that does not seem important right now. She smiles at me, expectation written on her features; without a word she puts her arm through mine in a possessive gesture. I say my goodbyes to the Father, who simply nods and smiles at me, and Nicola steers me down the corridor toward the rear of the building. I start to ask where we are going, but she anticipates my question, as any good parent would, and tells me there is a walled garden in back of the friary where we can sit and talk in the shade of the fruit trees. She wants to hear me recount what has happened. Also, she has something, she says, to tell me.

The garden is secluded and quiet. If anything, it is even more tranquil and quiet than the friary itself, with the exception of the joyful birds that are declaiming in the upper branches of the trees. There are several benches in the garden; one is close to the stucco wall that runs under the trees. It seems especially inviting, and we choose that one.

"So, Papa," my Nicola says, "I simply must know what happened in that room with you and Father Bernardino. I'm sorry, but I cannot wait!" At that moment I find that my feelings of love for my daughter well upward in my heart like the waters of a springtime brook that spill over its banks and flood the surrounding countryside, bringing life and renewal.

"Oh, my love, my beautiful *colomba* . . . how can I begin to tell you?" I say. I look at her and am quiet for a moment, recollecting my thoughts. "All right then, it is like this," and I recount my experience to her, letting my memories unfold like the pages of a book. Two books really—the one very familiar and known to me, but the other quite new, never before opened.

As we enter the room (I tell her) I see that this is where the Father is staying. There is a small bed, no more than a cot, against one wall; a pillow and a thin gray blanket rest on it. A square wood table the size of a small cart wheel sits between two sturdy wood chairs. A clutter of papers covers the table; an inkwell and an assortment of quills stand off to the side. Father Bernardino turns one of the chairs so that the two now face, and bids me take a seat.

We sit in silence, the Father's unflinching pale eyes holding my attention. He smiles at me, but doesn't say anything for the longest while. Finally, just as I am reaching the point of embarrassed frustration and anxiety, he speaks.

"I think that you have suffered a long time, my son. Can you tell me about it?" His query is made without demand; it is an invitation for me to open my heart to him.

His question brings with it the awareness that I have been tense during the whole journey to the friary, and that my chest carries that now-familiar sense of tightness. I try to relax, making a conscious effort to take in a breath before answering: "I will try, Father." A breath. "Yes, I will try."

Now that I am closer to him I can see how deep are the lines that form patterns across his face; those around the eyes and forehead seem etched into the skin, as in an engraving. His skin is the color of parchment, weathered, as though Father Bernardino spends much of his time outdoors—skin that I would expect to see on a ploughman or farmer. He is older than I thought. But it is his eyes that draw my attention: they are the palest shade of blue, not gray, as I had remarked last evening. They seem to see me with great clarity, as though looking straight into my soul. But they are also kind and understanding.

Previously, if someone asked me this question about my life, I would not give a forthright answer. I would hedge and skirt the issue. The whole history of my life is too painful to even try to begin. This is what I have done with Claudia in the past—minimize the seriousness of the situation, put it off and simply not address the matter. So my instinctive reaction when Father Bernardino asks this question is to go down the same well-worn path of denial and avoidance. But there is something kind in the set of his eyes, something that assures me it is now permissible to enter into the darkness of my soul. He will be there with me; it feels safe.

So I tell him my story, just as I did to you, Nicola, last night: the death of my mother; my father's decision to send me to my aunt and uncle; the fear and confusion I felt when parted from my family; living with the strange and fearsome uncle Bartolomeo. But then I go beyond what I had told you last night: I choose to enter into the indescribable terror of the nights, of not knowing if *zio* Bartolomeo would come into my room or not. I relate how, in the past several weeks and months—or is it longer?—I find that I am completely shipwrecked in my conception of time. My nights have been living hell on earth.

Father Bernardino leans toward me. "Every moment of terror in childhood is a month of nightmares in adulthood." He understands.

A reflective pause, then Father Bernardino says, "So you learned to hide." The penetrating gaze of the pale blue eyes holds me and doesn't waver, sending an unspoken message through their intensity. He isn't shocked or put off by the opening of my heart, the smell of decay that is part of my ancient wound.

"Hide? Hmm . . . yes, perhaps I did hide, in a sense. People have always known me as quiet, thoughtful—"

"And that," Father Bernardino says, "might have simply been a way of hiding *inside* yourself, if you understand my meaning?" He pauses and his gaze seems to bore into me with even more intensity. It is as if Father Bernardino is hunting something in me, tracking down that dark, shadowy interior place which has remained elusive, even to me, over these many years.

"Now my son, this is what must be done." Father Bernardino says this with authority, but also with great compassion. I know that he isn't commanding me—as well he could from his position of authority in the church—as much as suggesting, from a standpoint of spiritual wisdom and maturity, the necessary action.

"You must forgive your uncle."

I must have looked startled, because he says it again. But, to forgive him is—in my mind—unimaginable. How can I do that, after all that *zio* Bartolomeo has done to me?

"Yes," he says, "I know that the idea of forgiving someone like your uncle, someone who has inflicted great damage upon your heart, seems to you difficult, if not impossible. But consider this: the longer you refuse to let go of your hatred and pain toward him, the longer you will suffer, my son. Yes, it is *you* who will suffer the most!"

I look at Father Bernardino dumbfounded. What does he mean, it is I who will undergo the most suffering? I know my countenance reflects without a doubt the inner feelings and thoughts that roil in me; there is no hiding my shock and—yes, indignation. So he undertakes to explain.

Father Bernardino tells me the story found in the holy Gospel of Saint Matthew: our Lord compares two slaves serving in a king's palace to our situation here on earth. They—and we—have an immense debt toward God because of the incalculable destruction to our souls through sin, but are incapable of paying back that indebtedness

"So you see, my son," he continues, "God in His mercy forgave us our debt toward Him. It was paid through the sacrifice of His Son, our Lord Jesus, when He died on the cross."

"But Father," I protest, "my uncle is dead now; that was many years ago. Surely there can be nothing to accomplish by my forgiveness now?"

The beginning of a smile creeps onto his lips, but Father Bernardino is not mocking me. "Ah, my son, memories do not die in our lifetime; only when we do. Until that time, our past can haunt us as effectively as any malign spirit from the sulfurous pits of Hell."

I do not know what to make of this. Shall I forgive my uncle, and if so, for what? For the hurt he caused me, the terror of interminable waiting in that bed as a child, waiting for the unspeakable to happen again? I am aware that a part of myself—the greater part—doesn't want to forgive, but rather wants to hold on to the anger and bitterness that reside deep in my heart. Why should this man be let off without payment, I ask myself. I become lost in my thoughts and only when, after some moments, the Father speaks do I return to the present reality of this room.

"Forgiving someone is not a choice we have the luxury of granting or not, my son." Father Bernardino shakes his head with gravity, as if to say that he, too, has traveled down this path before. "Our Lord commands us to forgive, because it is for our sake, our health, that we do so."

I sit there, struggling with what he has told me. I feel ready to leave; what he asks is something too great, too heavy a burden for me to carry. I feel confused by his explanations, and now a tiredness sets into my bones, a physical weariness that presses me down in the chair like a profound weight.

Suddenly my thoughts turn to you, my little dove, my beloved daughter. No, don't blush! I seem to see your face before me: you are smiling your beautiful smile and looking at me. In this vision you are much younger than what you are today; you seem to be a young girl on the verge of embarking on the journey to womanhood. You are looking toward me in an expectant manner, about to ask me something; that is what I sense in my heart. But what do you want from me, what can I give you?

So gently that I hardly perceive it, I feel the light touch of Father Bernardino's hand as it rests on my knee. It is a touch of *connection*, reminding me that I am in the presence of another human being, someone who cares and who has reached out across the void of loneliness, of pain, someone who desires to inhabit this invisible bond. I feel the comfort and reassurance of his touch flow into me like the pouring of warm oil into my heart.

"Come, Holy Spirit of God," the priest whispers, then begins a prayer—not a written one, but words he is speaking from his heart to the Lord. As he prays, so softly that I am scarcely aware of his words, the image in my mind undergoes a change. You, Nicola, fade . . . but that is not accurate. How do I describe that which is indescribable? It is like the substance of morning light and fog, so frail and tenuous that I cannot be sure it is there at all. Nevertheless, I will endeavor to do so.

As your image fades—but no, it seems you are moving backward, farther away from me—someone else approaches and takes your place, walking in a slow and deliberate manner into the foreground of this scene I am watching. Yes, I am merely the spectator, not a participant. I am *there*, but also detached, removed from what I see, like you and I were last night standing on the steps outside the Duomo, looking on as the *falo* burned at a remove from us. I watch this scene, but now I want to call it a vision. All at once the person who is walking closer to me, taking a place right in front of me, is someone I recognize. It is our Lord.

How do I know? I cannot tell you how it was that I knew; I simply *knew*. When I mentioned this to Father Bernardino afterwards, he simply nodded; he also knew. "We call it a 'mystery,'" he said.

As I watch the scene, I am able to clearly and distinctly see our Lord. In this respect it is different from a dream one might have during the night, where vague shapes float across the rolling landscape of our minds. No, I see Him as I see Father Bernardino if I were looking at him, which I am not at this moment. At first Jesus stands there looking at me; He is neither smiling nor frowning; it's a look that a father has in the presence of his children.

But it is not what I see, but what I *feel* that is remarkable. No words are exchanged, no instructions or admonitions given; simply being with our Lord brings with it a melting away—yes, a flushing—of all the inner fears and terrors that I am carrying. Indeed, everything that previously worried and troubled me in my life is now absent. It is gone. I am aware of nothing else around me but our Lord, standing with me.

As I gaze at Him, I see a smile begin to form on His face, and gentle furrows appear at the corners of His mouth. Then He turns and beckons to someone behind Him; I cannot yet see this person. But Jesus is glad to see the person, as He is glad to be with me. Step by step I see this person approach and now I'm puzzled why he is included, so to speak, in this scene with Jesus.

It is my uncle, Bartolomeo. He stands beside our Lord, and he is smiling, something I never saw him do when he was alive. His face is peaceful, relaxed and content. As I look at him I am surprised to realize that my feelings of anger and resentment toward him are no longer there; they are gone. Somehow, in a way that I cannot understand or explain— even to myself—I can see my *zio* as the person God made him to be, without the inner pain that turned him into the rageful being I knew as a child. Then it is over. The vision disappears; not in a gradual way, not a fading away, not a dimming of light. One moment I see them, my uncle and Jesus together; the next moment the whole scene is gone and I am back in the room with Father Bernardino.

When I open my eyes (for I had them closed during the entire episode) the Father raises his head from prayer and opens his eyes, also. I smile at him. There are no words and for this moment I do not try to create them. It would be like talking during the solemn mass in church; that is how I perceive the atmosphere of holiness that fills the room where we sit.

As when we first entered the room and sat down, the Father and I simply remain in silence for what seems to be a long time, although in reality it is probably no longer than several minutes. I am at peace with the silence; my entire being feels at peace. It is a wonderful feeling, and I want to give voice to the joy I experience inside me, but I think that, also, would be inappropriate. So we sit.

Finally, Father Bernardino speaks. "Are you ready now to forgive your *zio*, my son?"

"I have already forgiven him, Father." The words come from my lips before the thought is formed. Strange, this pronouncement of mine! I know that I have released Uncle Bartolomeo, but I have no remembrance of having done so. Nevertheless, it is done and zio no longer troubles me.

I turn to Nicola sitting on the bench beside me; her gentle hand has been holding mine during the entire recounting. Quiet tears make their way down her pale cheeks, but her eyes are shining with love and joy. I understand that her tears are also mine, the ones I could not shed during those years of pain and agony in childhood. They are also Christ's, and therefore they are precious and healing.

"Oh, Papa, that's so beautiful! I am so happy for you," she says through her tears, which are still coursing down her face, dropping in small glistening globes to the dark earth alongside the bench. I move to wipe them away with my bare hand, but brush her nose instead. Nicola smiles at me, happy for her clumsy father.

We embrace, and then my daughter leans back and looks at me with sudden seriousness. So grown up, this *piccola colomba* of mine! I can tell she has something to tell me, a thing that weighs heavy on her heart.

"Papa, I have something to say," she begins; now she is my grave and subdued child. She glances in my eyes, then looks down at the ground for a moment, thinking of how to shape her words.

I raise my hand to her lips and gently cover her mouth. She draws back a little, surprised by her father's actions. "Yes, I know, I know," I say. "Father Bernardino has already told me. Do not blame him: he thought I needed to know before we tell your mother."

Nicola's eyes widen in astonishment; now our roles have reverted to their correct ones. She is the child; I am the parent, the one who teaches, corrects, and provides guidance, making the path she treads safe to follow.

"So . . . so you know," she stammers. I nod with affirmation.

"Yes, my *colomba*, I know. And I give you my blessing to enter the order of the Sisters of Mercy." Her eyes fill with tears, and like the river in springtime, begin overflowing their banks once again. So my little dove is to be betrothed after all, but to a Husband most unanticipated. "But, my love, know that this will be a great shock to your mother, so we must think together of how to tell her."

Now I am comfortable in my role as parent, helping to carry the happy burden my daughter has been struggling with these many weeks. Together we will think of a way to break this astounding, shocking, wonderful news to Claudia. But it will be all right; the Lord has already told me.

Christ be with me, Christ within me,
Christ behind me, Christ before me,
Christ beside me, Christ to win me,
Christ to comfort and restore me.
Christ beneath me, Christ above me,
Christ in quiet, Christ in danger,
Christ in hearts of all that love me,
Christ in mouth of friend
and stranger.

from "St. Patrick's Breastplate"
8th century Celtic prayer

About the author

Charles Ohrenschall grew up in California and currently lives in Georgia. He was a Navy pilot during the Viet Nam war, later an airline pilot, and then served with an international mission agency in Africa. He has an M.A. in counseling and in 1993 he and his wife founded Teleios Counseling Ministries. The Ohrenschalls have traveled extensively in Western Europe and have an on-going ministry in Russia. Their two adult sons and one grandson also live in Georgia.

If you have a comment about this book you'd like to share with the author, he may be contacted at:

WholeCloth14@gmail.com

Printed by CreateSpace, an Amazon.com Company

This book is available from Amazon.com and other retail outlets.